# DAN PRICE

# THE DIRTIEST ANGEL

## A MCBRIDE AND BUCKHOLTZ NOVEL

FOR ALL THE SEMINOLE INDIANS THAT CAME
BEFORE AND AFTER FREDDY SIMPSON, TEDDY
WELCH, JIMMY NELMS, AND HAL MOORE.  AND TO
THE CLASS OF 1965.  MAY GOD BLESS AND KEEP
YOU ALL.

# THE NEST GOES EMPTY

## CHAPTER ONE

Malcolm McBride sat in the floor playing with his grandson as Sheryl watched.  It had been a year since the death of Denise McBride, Sheryl's mother.  Denise McBride had been the binding tie that held the family together; and now she was gone, killed by a psychopath.  Even with the killer's death, there had been no closure.  Because of the death of her mother, Sheryl had asked for and been granted a leave from law school; but it was time to go back.  She watched as her father rolled Malcolm Junior over on his back, and she thought of all the family had endured.

"You keep tickling him I'm going to let you change his diaper."

"He's almost three.  He shouldn't be wearing a diaper," said Malcolm.

"I'll let you discuss that with him.  I'm sure he'll listen to his grandpa.  So, what do you guys want to eat?"

Sheryl watched Malcolm pick the baby up and throw him over his shoulder.  She almost fainted the first time he did that, but from the very first time the baby squealed with delight.  Like everyone else Sheryl knew, Malcolm Junior seemed to trust his grandfather completely.

"Hamburgers," said Malcolm.  "The men of the house demand hamburgers."

They followed Sheryl into the kitchen.  Anticipating exactly what Malcolm would say, she had already fixed the burgers.  The baby crawled up on Malcolm's shoulder and straddled his neck.  It made Malcolm look like a giant with a large tumor growing out of the top of his head.  The phone rang, and effortlessly he swung the baby over his shoulder and placed him gently on the floor.

"Yeah," said Malcolm.  "You sure?  Okay, I'm eating lunch with my daughter and grandson; I'll be there as soon as I can."

He hung up; and as if on cue, Malcolm Junior crawled back up in his lap.

"It was Arnie.  Captain Edwards says we have a case," said Malcolm.

Sensing his disappointment at having to leave, Sheryl knew it was time to let him know.

"Dad, we have to go back to Houston tomorrow.  I can't expect them to extend me anymore time."

"I know," he answered.

No more was said until the lunch was finished.  Malcolm went into the bedroom and dressed for work.

"You gonna leave early?" he asked as he tied his tie.

"Yes, the plane leaves at seven.  Maxine will be by about five to take us to the airport."

Malcolm nodded and bent down to hug his grandson one more time.

"Sheryl, I ......."

He lowered his head and turned toward the door.  She knew he was crying.  She ran to him and grabbed his arm.  Turning, he picked her up and crushed her to his chest.  No words were spoken.  Malcolm loved her, and she knew it.  He set her down and headed for the door.

# REMEMBER ME?

## CHAPTER TWO

When Malcolm arrived at the station, Arnie was already in Captain Edward's office.  Arnie Buckholtz was Malcolm's partner; and at forty-five, he was finally beginning to show his age.  Grey hair was growing around his temples.  At barely five eight and one hundred seventy pounds, he looked anything like what he was, a Golden Gloves Champion.  In contrast, Malcolm was six four and weighed two hundred fifty.  They made quite a lethal combination, and many in the criminal world had found that out the hard way.

"The FBI has a twelve-year-old child under protection."

He nodded toward two empty chairs.  The two detectives sat down.

"She's in an FBI Safe House.  According to our sources, there's a contract out on her for fifty thousand."

"Good Lord, what did she see?" said Malcolm.

"Jarvis Meadows," said Captain Edwards.

Malcolm and Arnie both looked at each other at the same time.

"Apparently he's not dead," said the captain to two shocked faces.  "Her name is Clarisse, and she saw him kill her mother and father.  Word on the street is that the father owed money to some people he couldn't pay.  Clarisse was hiding in a clothes hamper, and through a small hole she saw and heard everything.  The FBI had her sit down with a sketch artist, and then she was shown some photos that matched the sketch.  She picked out a guy that is supposed to have been dead for over a year."

Malcolm began to shake his head.

"I put two hollow point bullets in his chest.  Then he fell over a hundred-foot cliff into the bay.  There's no way he lived through that."

"I was there too, Captain.  Malcolm's right," said Arnie.

"I might be inclined to agree with you, but the body was never recovered.  That leaves room for argument."

Malcolm walked over to the glass window and stared out at the beehive of activity in the outer office.  Officers and detectives scurried everywhere all in an effort to try and keep a lid on a small area of crime overseen by the station house known as the two-four.  Sometimes it felt like they had been told to clear all the sand off the beach by hand.  You could pick up sand all day and still not make a dent in it.

Turning back, Malcolm said, "So what does any of this have to do with us?"

"Clarisse Mitchell specifically asked for you.  It seems you saved her life from a felon named Tony Cox."

Malcolm remembered.  Tony Cox had taken her hostage.  There was a firefight, and she was lucky to have survived.  But it was the SWAT team that saved her.  Nevertheless, his was the first face she saw; and she had clung to him like a life preserver.

"What's this?" said Malcolm as Captain Edwards handed him a piece of paper.

"It's the cell number of one of the agents guarding her.  She has demanded to talk to you.  This was the only way the FBI would allow it."

"A twelve-year-old demanded something from the FBI, and they agreed?"

"Apparently, Clarisse Mitchell is a twelve-year-old going on twenty-five.  With all she's seen and what has happened in her short life, I can see how she might have skipped most of her childhood stage."

Malcolm pointed toward the door, and Captain Edwards nodded.  He walked outside and dialed the number.

It rang one time.

"Yeah?" said a voice.

"This is Detective McBride of the two-four.  I was told Clarisse wants to talk to me."

A few seconds passed.

"Hello?" said a female voice.

"Clarisse, it's Detective McBride."

"You doing okay?" she said.

The question surprised him.

"I heard about your wife," she continued.  "I'm so sorry."

Her voice sounded like a child, but the words were those of a grown woman.  She had lost her parents and was running for her life, and yet she was concerned about Malcolm's state of mind.

"Thanks, Clarisse.  She was a good woman."

"You know my mom and dad are dead?"

"Yes, and I'm sorry."

"It seems that we've both lost a lot.  You saved my life awhile back; now I'd like to return the favor.  The agents here told me you had a run in with Jarvis Meadows.  I think I know where he might be."

It would have been impossible to know whether the two agents in the room or Malcolm were shocked more. Malcolm could hear an uproar over the end of the phone as the two agents began questioning Clarisse about what she'd just said.  In a few seconds, he heard her scream, "Shut up!" There was immediate silence.

"You still there?"

"Still here," answered Malcolm.

"Now as I was saying before these two Bozos jumped in, I'm pretty sure I know where he is."

"How so?" said Malcolm.

"Daddy put me in the clothes hamper and piled clothes on top of me.  I watched through a small hole, and I could see and hear......"

She stopped, and Malcolm knew she was fighting to keep from breaking down.  He could feel her pain.  Denise had been gone for over a year, but he fought to maintain his composure every time he thought of her.

"When he shot my parents, I heard him say, 'Let's get back to Howard's.  Happy Hour starts at four.'  Do you know what that means, Detective?"

"Yes," he answered, "and so do you."

"You go get him.  I'll tell these two in about ten minutes."

She hung up; and if the agents hadn't figured it out, Clarisse was about to be in an all-out war with the FBI.  She knew Jarvis Meadows would never forget Malcolm, so she was giving Malcolm a chance to end it.  There were probably ten Howard Johnson Motor Inns in the New York area but not that many close to the Mitchell house.  It had been twenty-four hours since the killings.  What were the chances that Jarvis Meadows would still be there?

Malcolm rushed back into the office and told Captain Edwards what Clarisse had just told him.  Within minutes, the SWAT team had been notified; and Arnie and Malcolm were out the door.

"Which Howard Johnson's is it?" said Arnie.

"It has to be Lincoln and Bayside," said Malcolm.  "Captain Edwards said it is the closest to the Mitchell house."

Arnie nodded and watched as Malcolm maneuvered through traffic at almost seventy miles an hour.  The FBI agents were not stupid.  They quickly figured it out.  Jarvis Meadows had a mountain of information needed to put several crime bosses away for a very long time, and the FBI needed it.  What they failed to understand, and what both Malcolm and Arnie knew, was that Jarvis Meadows would never be taken alive.  He was a cold-blooded killer who valued no one's life not even his own.  They hoped they would get there before the FBI, but they didn't.  The FBI was already on the scene and in command when the SWAT Team arrived.  Malcolm and Arnie climbed out of their car and watched as Lieutenant Pierson of the SWAT team walked over.

"They said this was their gig and for us to stand down."

"Well, let's see what they come up with," said Malcolm.

The FBI had the motel surrounded; but as time elapsed, it didn't take long for Malcolm to realize that Meadows was gone.

"He's not here," said Malcolm.  "He's too smart to hang around in one place for very long."

In about thirty minutes, an obviously frustrated agent came out the front door of the motel.  Seeing the two detectives, he walked over.

"If he tries to blame us, I may have to pop him," said Malcolm, as he watched the approaching agent.

"Agent Glover, you McBride?"

"That would be me," said Malcolm.

"I was told you have some history with the suspect.  Is that true?"

"Yes, we have met before."

"Clarisse Mitchell, you know her too?"

"Yes."

"As of an hour ago, she fired her guards."

Malcolm laughed.

"Exactly how does a twelve-year-old fire the people who are protecting her?"

Agent Glover smiled.

"She fired Agents Lawrence and Bell.  She's a piece of work, isn't she?"

"I'm becoming more educated all the time," said Malcolm.  "So, what are you going to do with her?"

"Well, she'll do whatever I tell her.  But Captain Edwards and I have decided that things would go smoother if you and your partner would take over the protection detail."

Malcolm quickly looked at Arnie and then back at Agent Glover.

"Not happening!" said Malcolm.

Agent Glover laughed.

"Actually, it is.  Here's the address.  The agents are waiting for you."

Agent Glover walked away waving his hand in a circle indicating it was time to mount up and go home.

Malcolm held the paper as if he'd just been told he had some kind of terminal illness.  He looked at Arnie and back at the paper.  Head bowed, shoulders slumped, he turned and climbed in the car.

As Arnie called Maxine, his wife, to tell her of the situation, Malcolm continued staring straight ahead as if in a trance.  As they pulled up to the house, Malcolm checked his watch while shaking his head.

"It's almost six o'clock."

Before he could say what was on his mind, the front door of the house opened and out marched Clarisse.  It was nearly ten seconds before the first agent came running down the steps in pursuit.

"It's six o'clock.  I didn't think you guys were ever gonna get here. You guys hungry?"

She stood there with her arms across her chest asserting total control over the situation.  The first agent rushed up and began to try to explain how a witness with a price on her head was able to walk out the front door unprotected.  Malcolm raised his hand as he climbed out of the car.

"Save it agent. You Lawrence or Bell?"

Not waiting for an answer, Malcolm waved his hand signaling everyone to head back in the house.

"You're mad, aren't you?" said Clarisse, as she walked beside Malcolm.

"Yes," said Malcolm.  "These agents are perfectly capable of protecting you.  Detective Buckholtz has a wife and child and needs to be ........"

He stopped midsentence realizing he was about to say something stupid.  These agents probably had wives and kids too.  Being cooped up with a twelve-year-old would not have been their first choice of assignments, especially since it might be weeks before Jarvis Meadows was caught or killed.

Shaking his head, Malcolm said, "I'm sorry, we'll take it from here."

The detectives shook their hands and were seen to the door.

"Good luck, Detective," said one.

"Thanks," said Malcolm.

Clarisse walked back into the living room from the kitchen carrying an extra-large pizza still in the box.

"I've been warming it in the oven," she said.

She placed it on the coffee table and went back in the kitchen.  In a few minutes, she came back with three cups and a liter of coke.

"It's six o'clock, let's eat!"

# INTRODUCTION OF A KILLER

## CHAPTER THREE

As he cleaned his knife, Jarvis Meadows stared down at the body of Regan Knight. Criminals like Regan always became a liability at some point because of their stupidity. Clarisse Mitchell was alive and had seen and heard everything. Jarvis had given a simple order. Check the bathroom. Even with the life of his wife threatened, Seth Mitchell refused to give up the location of his daughter. There were a lot of places a kid could hide, and it would take hours to search them all. Realizing that Clarisse could hear everything, he warned her that her mother would be shot if she didn't show herself. When she didn't show, Jarvis shot Elise Mitchell in the head hoping that Clarisse would cry out or make some noise that would give away her location. Surely, she wouldn't let her father die too. But she did. With both parents' dead, they began to go through the house room by room. Regan was told to check the bathroom, but he didn't. While waiting for the Mitchells to give up the location of their daughter, Link Barlow had gone in to use the bathroom. The odor was so bad that Regan just opened the door and looked in. If he'd checked the clothes hamper, he would have easily found Clarisse. As they all met back in the living room, Regan said, "Let's go to Howard's. Happy Hour starts at four."

Jarvis knew that wherever Clarisse was she had heard that.  Whether she was smart enough to figure it out or not, Jarvis was taking no chances.  He ordered everyone to the car.  With Jarvis sitting in the back seat, Link drove; and Regan sat in the passenger side.

"Turn in at the next alley entrance," said Jarvis.

Link drove into an alley, and Jarvis reached across the seat and grabbed Regan by the hair.  Pulling his head back, he ran the knife across his throat.  As shocked as he was, Link still reached across, opened the passenger door, and pushed Regan's body out.  Jarvis had gotten out and was now staring at what was left of Regan Knight.

"People who allow their mouths to overload their brains don't live long.  You understand my meaning?"

Link's face had turned ashen, but he nodded.  Jarvis Meadows nodded too.  Pointing at Knight's body, Meadows said, "Clean this up!"

# CORNERED

## CHAPTER FOUR

"I want the iron," said Clarisse as they all sat down.

"I figured," said Malcolm.

"Why's that?" said Clarisse.

"Women keep house, they do the cleaning, naturally they'd want the iron."

"I'll take the hat," said Arnie.

"I've already got dubs on the hat," said Malcolm.

"I didn't hear you say anything about dubbing the hat?" said Arnie.

Ignoring Arnie's protest, Malcolm reached over and placed the hat on the board.

"So that leaves me with the shoe," said Arnie.

"Quit whining and roll the dice," said Clarisse.

Arnie rolled the dice, and one went off the board onto the carpet.

"Gotta roll again," said Malcolm.  "The dice have to be on the board when they stop rolling."

"Whose rule is that?" said Arnie.  "I've played a million times and never heard that one.  You made that up."

Clarisse sat back against the sofa and watched. Although only twelve, she had already picked up on the fun that these two had with each other.  In about thirty minutes of laughing, her stomach was beginning to hurt.  Play continued past midnight.

"Time's up," said Malcolm.

"You're broke," said Arnie.  "You're quitting because you can't afford to land on Boardwalk again."

"I'm quitting because I'm tired, and this thing over here, pointing at Clarisse, can barely keep her eyes open."

"We're supposed to play until somebody wins," protested Clarisse.

"That would be me," said Arnie.

"Okay, just leave everything right where it is; and we'll pick up right here tomorrow," said Malcolm.

Looking at Clarisse, he said, "It's time for you to hit the hay."

Before Malcolm could move, Clarisse jumped up and threw her arms around his neck.  Kissing him on the cheek, she disappeared down the hall and into her room. Malcolm stole a quick glance at Arnie who was about to make a comment.

"Women like Irish men."

"McBride is Scottish," said Arnie.

"More History Channel education?"

Before Arnie could reply, there was a knock at the front door.  Immediately, the two detectives drew their guns and moved to the side of the room.

"Who is it?" yelled Malcolm.

"Agent Lawrence," came the reply.

Arnie carefully pulled up one end of the blind and nodded to Malcolm.

"You alone?" said Malcolm.

"I'm alone."

Standing off to one side, Malcolm slowly opened the door.  As the agent came in, Malcolm briefly stepped out on the porch and looked up and down the street.  Seeing nothing suspicious, he walked back in and locked the door.

"What's going on?" said Arnie.

"Agent Bell's been killed."

The detectives quickly looked at each other.

"And you're here because?" said Malcolm.

"He was tortured."

Malcolm walked back over to the window and carefully lifted one corner of the blind and scanned the street.

"You and Bell have been gone for six hours, and you're telling us that in that period of time somebody kidnapped and tortured your partner?"

Arnie and Malcolm both knew what the death of Agent Bell meant.  The Safe House had been compromised.  Malcolm nodded toward Arnie.

"Call Captain Edwards.  Tell him we're moving Clarisse now."

"Where will you go?" said Agent Lawrence.

"I'll know when we get there," said Malcolm.

Malcolm raced down the hallway and knocked on Clarisse's bedroom door.  In less than five minutes, they were packed and ready to go.  The first one outside was Agent Lawrence.  As he ran toward his car, a black van pulled up.

"It's too late," he yelled; and then died in a hail of gunfire.

The back doors to the van opened, and four armed men emerged.  Malcolm quickly closed and locked the front door.

"Captain Edwards says the SWAT team is ten minutes away," said Arnie.

"We'll all be dead in ten minutes," said Malcolm. "Backdoor!"

With Clarisse and Arnie right behind him, they ran through the kitchen.

"They haven't had time to get around back," said Malcolm leading them down the steps.

As they sprinted across the back yard, flashlight beams began to emerge around the side of the house.

"Go!" said Arnie.

Malcolm and Clarisse opened the back gate and began to run down the alley.  They hadn't gone fifty yards when the sounds of gunfire made Malcolm stop.

"Arnie is by himself," said Malcolm.

"We've got to go back," said Clarisse.

Malcolm looked down the alley and then back at Clarisse.

"No," he said.  "The Calvary is on the way.  Arnie will hold 'em."

Four against one was no "hold em" numbers, and Malcolm knew Arnie wasn't going to live.  Cursing under his breath, they continued to run down the alley and out into a cross street.  He had no idea where they were.  The Safe

House was completely off the radar as to his familiarity with the area.

"Come on," he said.

It was one o'clock in the morning. All the streets were deserted. In a few seconds, he realized they were running down a dead-end street.

"Malcolm!" screamed Clarisse.

Turning, Malcolm saw the van coming around the corner.

"Run!" she screamed leading the way across the street toward a corner house. At two hundred fifty pounds, Malcolm wasn't quick or agile; but he followed her lead. Luckily, she had picked the only house whose wooden fence didn't mesh completely with the side. The gap was wide enough for Clarisse, but Malcolm soon widened it smashing through like a knife through butter. As they ran across the backyard, Clarisse stumbled. All in one motion, Malcolm picked her up and literally threw her across his shoulder. They reached the gate to the back fence just as the killers burst through Malcolm's hole. Almost tearing the gate off its hinges. Malcolm raced out into the woods that surrounded the dead-end street. It was pitch black, and it was only a matter of time before he would trip. When it came, they were about a hundred yards away from their pursuers. Malcolm stepped in a hole. As he went down, Clarisse flew over his shoulder and crashed onto the ground knocking her unconscious.  Crawling to where she lay, he picked her up, and then realized he'd twisted his ankle badly.  He fell back to the ground cradling Clarisse in his arms and saw the flashlights coming fast.  He couldn't tell if they'd been spotted, and he couldn't take the chance.  He gritted his teeth and forced himself to stand.  Every step was agony as he made his way toward what looked to be the thickest of the trees and underbrush.  Forcing his way through, he stumbled.  He gently laid Clarisse on the ground.  It was time to fight.  He pulled his Glock and lay down facing the sounds of the pounding feet.  In just a few minutes, he could hear voices and see the flashlights beginning to search the ground.

"You see footprints?" said Link.

"Yeah, but only one set.  The big guy must be carrying her," said Raymond.

"Looks like they headed this way," said Abbott, pointing toward the heaviest of the vegetation.

"He's armed. Why hasn't he used it?" said Link.

"The girl, you idiot.  He knows firing will give away his position," said Abbott.

"So, what are we gonna do?  The cops will be all over this place in a few minutes," said Link.

"Burn 'em out.  It's all dead brush.  Link, you and Abbott go about fifty yards to the left.  Start a fire about every fifteen feet.  I'll do the same," said Raymond.

Malcolm heard every word; and as he felt the grass against his hands and face, he knew just how dry it was.  They had to get deeper into the woods.  As quietly as he could, he picked Clarisse up and willed himself to walk away from what he knew would soon be a raging inferno.

----- ----- -----

Arnie had been shot.  He pulled himself behind a steel dumpster but then realized he was about to be surrounded.  He broke through the wood fence behind the dumpster and crawled into the backyard.  Now he was able to return fire from several different angles with the killers not knowing exactly where he was.  He'd taken a bullet to his shoulder, and it was bleeding badly.  He heard the sirens of the SWAT team, and apparently the killers had too.  The sounds of them running down the alley could be heard as well as the crunch of gravel against the van's tires as it pulled around.  There were five of them.  Somebody had stayed in the van.  Arnie sat down and lay back against the board fence.  In a few seconds, he could hear voices and see light coming from the Safe House backyard.  He yelled for help.

# HELL FIRE

## CHAPTER FIVE

In minutes, the sky was ablaze.  The fire began to explode jumping from tree to tree.  Malcolm didn't have to look back. He could feel the heat of the inferno on his back. The adrenaline was coursing through his body like a river through a broken dam.

Clarisse was still unconscious.  The thought that the killers were still in pursuit had become secondary.  He ran down into a gulley and nearly fell.  He spied an open field on the other side that was almost barren of vegetation.  When he reached it, he stopped and looked back for the first time. He didn't know how far he'd come; but as he looked around, he could see he'd run into a ravine with sheer rock cliffs on both sides rising several hundred feet.  They were completely blocked in.  There was nowhere to go but straight ahead.  He sat down and carefully lowered Clarisse to the ground.  She groaned and opened her eyes.

"Malcolm!"

"I'm right here."

"Where are we?"

"Good question.  I had no idea New York State had anything that could still be considered wilderness, but we're in it."

Clarisse sat up and looked around.  The fire was still coming but had slowed considerably as it hit the open field.

"And I don't know where we're going to go," said Malcolm anticipating her next question.  "For now, we've got to stay ahead of the fire.  How do you feel?"

She nodded.

"Try and stand."

Using his shoulder for a brace, she stood up.

"A little dizzy, but I'm okay.  You?"

Malcolm glanced down at his right ankle which looked like it had a tumor growing out the side.  The adrenaline rush was over as signaled by the pain beating a rhythm with the pounding of his heart.  He sat down.

Clarisse saw his ankle and knelt, carefully lowering his sock.

"I've been shot, beaten up, and stabbed.  I think I can survive a twisted ankle.  Now help me up."

Pretending to put his full weight on her shoulders, Malcolm balanced himself and began to limp toward the darkness and uncertainty of what lay ahead.

The SWAT team found nothing but Arnie at the scene and quickly yielded to the hundreds of fire department personnel that began to arrive.  Ignoring Arnie's demands to wait until Malcolm and Clarisse could be found, they took him to the hospital.

Captain Edwards was waiting when Arnie arrived.  As they wheeled him into surgery, Arnie told Captain Edwards everything that happened.  Someone had told Jarvis Meadows of the location of the Safe House.  The same thing had happened two years before with a crime lord named Anthony Bazzani.  Someone in the FBI was dirty.

# DESPERATE

## CHAPTER SIX

Another hour passed, and the light from the fire became hidden behind the walls of rock that towered all around them.  Malcolm was in real trouble, and he knew it.  Not only was he completely lost, but he had a twelve-year-old with him.  And now the pain from his ankle had reached the point that he couldn't go on.

"Let's rest over here for awhile," he said.

Clarisse knew he was hurting.  She had felt his muscles contract throughout his body with each and every step.  She sat down with him pretending to be grateful for the rest.  The sky was clear, and the light from the moon illuminated their surroundings.

"I don't guess you have a clue as to where we are?" she said.

"Not a clue," he said.

Standing up, she walked over about twenty feet and stared up at the cliff wall.  She noticed a small stream of water trickling down.  Reaching out, she caught it in her hand and began to drink.  When the water hit her empty stomach, she remembered it had been more than eight hours since the pizza.

Walking back, she said, "Can you move?"

"Move where?"

"There's water over here.  If I had something to catch it, I'd bring it to you."

Malcolm could barely spit.  He rolled over on his knees and crawled over.

"You remind me of Elmo."

Malcolm finally got to the wall and began to catch the water in his mouth.

"Who's Elmo?"

"My three-legged dog.  The people at the Pound were gonna put him down, but I told 'em I'd take him.  He actually got around really good."

"You still got him?"

"No, with only three legs he couldn't outrun a truck."

"I'm sorry."

Malcolm crawled over and put his back against the wall.

"Clarisse, I'm afraid I'm through for awhile. "

He rolled up his pants leg and looked at his ankle.  It was swollen twice its normal size.

She immediately got up and started walking along the wall following the water.

"Where are you going?" said Malcolm.

"Not far."

In a few seconds, she rounded a corner and was out of sight.  Malcolm waited another minute and then became concerned.

"Clarisse!" he yelled.

She didn't respond, so he yelled several more times but got no answer.  Using the wall, he pulled himself up balancing on his left foot.  He began to hop in the direction she'd gone.  He hopped about ten feet and fell hard breaking his arm.  It was over.  He couldn't pull himself back up, and he couldn't crawl.

----- ----- -----

Maxine and Captain Edwards stood in the doorway watching Arnie try to button his shirt with one hand.

"Where do you think you're going?" said Maxine.

Arnie looked up and shook his head.

"I don't want to hear it.  The bullet went straight through.  They've stitched it up. I've got a bottle of pain pills and antibiotics.  Malcolm and Clarisse are in trouble.  Jarvis Meadows is not going to rest until they're dead."

"I've got helicopters combing a twenty-mile radius of where they were when the fire started.  There are over one hundred National Guard troops on the ground; and as soon as the fire area cools down, they'll start searching that area too.  There's nothing you can do, Arnie."

Arnie sat down on the edge of the bed.

"We had to leave so quick he didn't take his cell phone.  All he has is his Glock and one clip.  Meadows will have fifty people looking for him."

Captain Edwards walked over and pulled up a chair.

"There's nobody better at adapting and gaining control of a situation than Malcolm."

"If he wasn't trying to protect a twelve-year-old girl, what you're saying could be true.  But if one is hurt, his options are seriously reduced.  And God help both of 'em.  If the killers don't get to 'em, nature will."

----- ----- -----

"You see the choppers?" said Raymond, squinting through a rising sun,

"I see 'em," said Meadows.  "I saw the National Guard too.  It won't make any difference.  Take half the men and go into the park."

"What about the park rangers?"

"They won't be out this late.  Tell Abbott to circle around to the Appalachian Trail and come back this way."

Meadows spread a map across the hood of the Jeep.

"They went in here.  The Appalachian Trail starts about twenty miles north.  Since we can't go in from this end, we'll go in the back way."

"What makes you think they'll head for the Trail?"

"There's nothing but a canyon from here to the park entrance. No way out except up cliffs on both sides.  They don't have climbing gear."

"Okay."

"One more thing," said Meadows.  "When you find 'em, call me.  The detective's mine.  Kill the girl, but McBride is mine.  Understand?"

"I understand."

# SIMON LEGREE

## CHAPTER SEVEN

Clarisse had finally found it.  She had walked over three hundred yards following the trickle of water hoping it would end somewhere in a pool.  There it was a small basin holding about two gallons.  She turned around and began to retrace her steps.  When she saw Malcolm, he was still sitting with his back against the wall.

As she walked up, he said, "I was getting worried." He held his right arm down so she couldn't see it had begun to swell too.

"I had to find a place where the water pooled.  You need to stick your ankle in it."

"Too late for that," he said.  "It's as swollen as it's going to get.  I can't stand on it."

"Yes, you can.  Use me for a crutch.  We've got to get to the water."

She took the strips of cloth and soaked them in the water coming down the rocks.  Gently, and carefully, she began to wrap them around his swollen ankle.  The cold water felt good, and he leaned back and closed his eyes.  She tied the strips in a Granny Knot, the only knot she knew how to tie. It was effective. The pain immediately changed from a stabbing sensation to an ache.

"I'll be right back," she said.

Malcolm started to protest but knew it would do no good.  She disappeared around the corner.  Following the rock wall, she found the pool of water and began to look around.  There was little light but enough for her to see what she needed. She continued to follow the water trail.  In another few minutes, she heard the sound of water rushing.  The trickling stream had combined with others to form one much wider.  She began to follow it until she heard the waterfall.  The water spilled down an overhang cascading somewhere below.  She spied a small dirt path off to the side. Not knowing where it led, she decided to follow it. It wound down the cliff face for about fifty feet and then angled back toward the falls.  The moon was just at the right spot to illuminate what looked like an open area behind the falls.  She climbed up to inspect.  Sure enough, there was a cave in the rock.  This was where she and Malcolm could hide.  And like it or not, he was coming even if she had to drag him.

Malcolm heard her running long before she came into view.

"Are you crazy.  If you fall, you'll break every bone in your body."

"I'm a lot tougher than you are, Mister."

She knelt beside him and spotted the arm.

"I can't leave you alone five minutes and you go and hurt something else?"

"What can I say?  I'm falling apart."

"Well, I found a place for us to hide.  We can't stay here."

"Clarisse...."

"Shut up, Malcolm.  I don't want to hear it.  I've been kidnapped, shot at, seen my parents murdered, and now I'm being chased through the forest by killers.  I'm mad, and I want you to get mad.  Now get up.  Use me for a crutch.  We'll go slow, but we're going!"

Malcolm looked at the determination in Clarisse's eyes. She was in charge, and the more he thought about it, the angrier he got.

"Help me up, Simon Legree."

"Who's that?"

"I'll tell you later."

————————

Seth Abbott and four men were on the Appalachian Trail moving steadily toward the park entrance.  Because of the fire, the ranger stations were all manned which had caused problems.  To elude detection, they had to find paths off the main trail, and that had slowed them down considerably.  They'd covered about five miles.  It was almost noon.  There would be no eluding detection now.  If spotted, the rangers would have to be killed; and Meadows would not want that.  They were all equipped with automatic weapons and rifles with scopes.  They had enough food for three days; but Abbott knew that if the girl wasn't found in two, Meadows would be furious.  After taking a five-minute break, they hit the trail again, this time at a jogging pace.  In about thirty minutes, Abbott called a halt for a water break.

"The entrance to the park is about a mile," said Raymond.  "I used to come up here with my dad when I was a kid."

Abbott consulted the map.

"What's the best way around the ranger station?"

"Circle as wide as you can.  Most of the rangers will be out on their patrols.  There shouldn't be any or very few around the station house.

"What about our weapons?"

"Leave 'em here.  I will circle around and meet you on the other side of the park entrance.  It will be a lot easier for one man to get by than four."

"Okay, we'll do what Raymond suggests. Get your backpacks and leave your hardware here," said Abbot

# DUB SMITH

## CHAPTER EIGHT

Royce Chambers and Rage came out of the cabin and stretched.  The morning stretch for Rage involved a large poop and watering the foliage.  The two had lived up in the mountains in sight of the Appalachian Trail, known as the AT, for nearly ten years.  The forest provided what they needed for shelter and food; and when winter came, they had a nice warm cabin already stocked with firewood and food.  As he sat down and looked across the endless forest, his thoughts once again went back to a family long gone. The day Betsy died, Chambers killed the admitting nurse and two orderlies.  Betsy was only ten, and they refused her admittance because there was no insurance on file.  Chambers didn't have time to pick hospitals.  Betsy had gone into insulin shock, and Rice Memorial was the closest hospital.  She was all he had left.  Her mother, Brenda, had died two years earlier of Ovarian Cancer.  It had been a slow and agonizing death.  The "system", as Chambers began to call it, took care of the ones who could pay; and the others.... well, the others be damned.  Brenda had been given the needed treatment, but the cancer had just been too aggressive.  And the arrogance and disinterest shown when he brought his daughter in the emergency room would not be tolerated.  She had died in his arms while the admittance nurse tried to make him fill out paperwork.  His years as a boxer along with his rage and grief sent him over the edge.  He reached across the counter and literally pulled the woman through the window breaking her neck.  When the two orderlies came through the door, he hit one so hard his facial bones were shoved into his brain.  The other one tried to run, but Chambers slammed him headfirst into the wall breaking his neck.  It was over in a matter of seconds.  He looked at the bodies and then at the waiting room full of stunned and horrified faces.  Gathering Betsy in his arms, he ran out the emergency room door.  He'd eluded capture for ten years.  All the years of camping with his father had given him knowledge of the forest that had kept him safe.  Of course, he knew, at some point, he would die either at the hands of the authorities, when they finally found him, or from the many lethal elements all around him.  Either way, it didn't matter.

As the sun broke through the trees, he noticed movement down below, movement that was two legged not four.  He could see the AT from his cabin, and it was rare that anyone would dare venture away from it.  But whoever this this trail blazing back packer was, he was making an obvious effort to avoid the ranger station.  Looking through his binoculars, he saw the armory the man was carrying four rifles all fitted with scopes.  He quickly checked the AT but saw nothing.

"What do you think, Rage? Are they after us?"

The wolf trotted over and knelt at Chamber's feet. Whether genetic or not, he never howled unless danger was close, be it human, or one nature provided.  Chambers continued to watch as the man skirted around and behind some large rocks located at the base of the Fire Tower.  The ranger in the tower was not searching the ground below, or he would have easily seen the movement.  During the night Chambers spotted the fire, but it had been contained.  There were several fire breaks built in the forest miles away from the park entrance.  There had never been any danger of it getting this far.  It took the man nearly thirty minutes to traverse the rugged terrain, but he finally climbed out of the ravine and back on the AT.  Almost at the same time, three men appeared walking out of the park entrance.  There was a verbal exchange, and the weapons were handed out.  Chambers knelt and scratched the wolf's ears.

"They aren't after us, old buddy.  But they're seriously after someone.  Besides us, who are they after that would require that kind of firepower?"

----- ----- -----

Malcolm suddenly jerked and opened his eyes.  As he frantically looked around, it took him several seconds to remember where he was.  He glanced over at Clarisse who was still sound asleep.

*"Thank God she didn't catch me napping," he thought.*

It had to be nearly mid-day.  He painfully rolled over on his side and pushed himself up with his one good arm.  He was thirsty and way past hungry.  With only one hand to pull himself up, he slowly made his way over to the fall.  Water had pooled in some of the rock depressions.  He pushed his face into the water and drank.  In a few seconds, he felt as if he'd drunk a gallon which presented the next problem.  He had to pee.  With Clarisse still asleep, he crawled back to the wall and pulled himself up.  There was no way to quietly hop outside; so, if she woke up, he'd just have to tell her to stay put. Nature was calling or something to that effect.  He made it just outside the entrance and spied some foliage that was in desperate need of water.  The relief he felt was at least a respite from the incessant pain from his foot and arm.  He looked around at the beautiful day.  The temperature was in the seventies. He could see the sky was a beautiful azure blue, and then he saw the four-armed men coming down the ravine.

"Clarisse!"

She jumped but made no sound.  The look on Malcolm's face told her all she needed to know.

"Get as far back in the corner as you can."

Malcolm lay down on his belly and waited.  The thundering of the waterfall drowned out their approach. One minute turned into two and then three.  Slowly, he crawled over to the entrance and peeked out.  They had passed. Crawling back, he said, "We're still safe for awhile."

"They'll be back," said a voice from somewhere in the dark.

Clarisse ran to Malcolm and knelt at his feet.

"I mean you no harm," said the voice.  "I saw them head this way, and I knew carrying all that armory they had some serious intentions."

Malcolm still could not tell where the voice was coming from; but he and Clarisse were now both lying down, Malcolm's gun aimed into the darkness.

"Who are you?" said Malcolm.

"My name serves no purpose.  But what I can offer you is a way out.  If it were you alone, I wouldn't care; but you have a child.  Is she yours?"

"That's none of your business.  Now you need to show yourself, or I'm going to start shooting."

"Number one, you won't shoot in an enclosed area like this; and number two, those men after you will see signs that you have come this way.  They'll turn around and start looking closer.  Now you've got two choices.  Put the gun down, and I'll help you get out of here, or wait until they get here.  Trust me, when they start firing, it won't make any difference that they can't see.  The ricocheting bullets will kill both of you."

Malcolm took a deep breath and looked at Clarisse.

"If he'd wanted to kill us, he could have done it five minutes ago.  What do you think?"

"You care what I think?" said Clarisse.

"Yesterday I didn't, but you've proven your worth now. It's your neck same as mine."

"Mr.?" said Clarisse.

"I hear you."

"Those men are after me.  I witnessed the murder of my mom and dad."

"They do the killing?" said the voice.

"No, but they're working for the man who did."

There were a few seconds of silence and slowly a figure materialized out of the darkness.

"My name's Dub Smith.  Who are you?"

———————

"There's a handprint.  He knelt here for water," said Raymond.

"Where did you get all this tracking expertise?" said Abbott.

"Boy Scouts, asshole.  I was in the Boy Scouts until my old man became an alcoholic.  I was just about to qualify as an Eagle when he lost his job, and we had to move.  Never did get back in it."

"That's really touching, but how do you know the handprint belongs to McBride?"

"Put your hand on the print."

Abbott knelt and placed his hand over the print.  The print was a size bigger.

"That's a big man's hand.  It's his, and they're headed back where we just came from.  Let's go."

As they retraced their steps, Raymond spotted several overturned rocks and finally saw a footprint.  He knelt and examined it.

"It's hers."

They all looked closely and could see how small it was.  Looking around, they saw was nothing but a canyon of rock sprinkled with trees.

"No place for them to hide here.  There must be a cave or something that would shelter them.  We would have seen them by now," said Raymond.

They continued and soon arrived at the falls.  As they came down the ravine, Raymond spotted the trail.  He quickly lowered his rifle and headed up.

"You see something?" said Abbott.

Raymond motioned them to be quiet and snaked his way across the rock face until he came to the entrance behind the falls.  Carefully, he peered in, and then walked inside.  In a few seconds, he motioned the rest to come up.

"They were here," he said as the others arrived.  "They made a bed out of a pile of leaves, and there are footprints everywhere."

He began to search the area with his flashlight. Kneeling, he shined the beam on another set of prints.

"What is it?" said Abbott.

"Moccasins."

# SAFE HAVEN

## CHAPTER NINE

Clarisse had never wavered.  When Smith, or whatever his name was, said, "Follow me if you want to live," she got down on her hands and knees and crawled through the hole in the back of the cave.  A large rock had hidden it from view.  They crawled in total darkness for nearly fifty feet before they could see light.  Malcolm's big body had barely made it out.  That had been over an hour ago.  Smith had never uttered another word.  Upon leaving the falls, they had started up a steep embankment and began following what appeared to be a deer path that disappeared and reappeared as they continued to climb.  Soon, they were above the tree line; and the wind was much colder.  If not for their dire circumstances, the view of the AT and the mountains on all sides would have been breathtaking.  As it was, fatigue combined with hunger, made all their beautiful surroundings nothing but a jail cell absent of the bars.  As they continued to climb, Malcolm knew Clarisse couldn't go much farther.  The wooden crutch that Smith had quickly made for him was digging into his armpit so hard that he could feel the blister forming.  As if attune to their agony, Smith stopped and pointed to a small rock basin full of rainwater.  Clarisse sat down and began to drink.

For the first time, Malcolm took time to study their rescuer.  He was dressed all in buckskin with a beard that nearly reached his belt.  Malcolm estimated him to be about forty.  Deep wrinkles brought on by the relentless sun were forming around a pair of slate blue eyes. He had a round face, bushy eyebrows, and a wide nose, sitting atop a frame of about a hundred and fifty pounds.

"How did you know about the cave?" said Malcolm.

"Been up here ten years.  There's not a rock or cave, as you call it, that I haven't been in."

Malcolm tried to process why someone would be up in the mountains for ten years but was too exhausted to worry about it.

"Where are we going?"

"Somewhere they can't find her," he said pointing at Clarisse.

When Smith saw Malcolm's gun back in the cave, he knew immediately that he was a cop or detective.  He almost turned and ran, but Betsy flashed into his mind.  He couldn't save her, but maybe he could this child.  He still wasn't sure what he was going to do with Malcolm, but up to this point it was evident that he cared about the child.  He had obviously been ready to risk his life for her, so that in itself was one point in his favor.  He walked over to the edge of the cliff and began to search the horizon.  He could see for several miles;

and with his binoculars, he was able to zero in on any activity behind them.  There was nothing yet.  Turning, he could see that Malcolm was in worse shape than the girl.  He hadn't noticed the arm at first, but now he could see it clearly.  The wrist and arm were angled.  If it wasn't straightened soon, it might never be used again.  But whatever had to be done couldn't be done here.

"Okay, let's go."

Struggling to his feet, Malcolm almost fell, but Smith caught him.

"You need to lose some weight," said Smith.

"Yeah, I've been told that several times.  I'll get right on that as soon as I get back from this mountain climb."

Smith had to smile.

*"I hope I don't have to kill this guy." he thought.  "He has a rare sense of humor. "*

Malcolm glanced at his watch as they descended into a thickly wooded area.  It was almost three o'clock.  Suddenly, as if walking through a door, they walked into a clearing with a cabin sitting in the middle of it.

"Home," said Smith.

He whistled, and a wolf came bounding around the cabin headed straight for them.  Malcolm dropped to his knees and reached for his gun, but it was obvious that the animal belonged to Smith.  He was huge.

"This is Rage," said Smith.  "I raised him from a pup."

With no further comment, Smith walked up to the cabin and went inside.  Malcolm and Clarisse looked at each other and followed.

----- ----- -----

It was obvious that the arm was hurting, but Arnie had never said a word.  Most of the National Guard had left, but several had been asked to stay because of their familiarity with the forest area.  It had not taken long to find where Malcolm and Clarisse had gotten water.  As with their pursuers, the handprint and shoeprint indicated that Malcolm and Clarisse were headed toward the park.  Logan Bernard, one of the guardsmen, nodded toward Arnie.

"The arm giving you trouble?"

"I'm okay," came the reply.  "So, they escaped the fire.  Any idea which direction they went?"

"There's not but one direction, Detective.  They had to go straight ahead.  It's going to be too dark to track in another hour."

The conversation was interrupted by a helicopter coming into view.  In what little open ground there was, the pilot was able to maneuver and set down.  It was Captain Edwards.

"What have you found?" he said running over to the group.

"Nothing except they're both still alive," said Arnie.

"Captain Edwards, I'm Logan Bernard.  You and the detective might want to look at this."

Walking back over to where the hand and shoeprint were found, Logan pointed to another set of prints.

"Four men."

He counted the prints and walked down about ten feet.

"They're tracking too.  I figure about four hours ahead of us.  Everything points toward the park area."

"Is there any place to land other than the Ranger Station?" asked Captain Edwards.

"No, Sir," said Logan.  "It gets pretty rough from here."

"How's the arm holding up?" said the captain.

"It hurts, but I'm okay."

"Alright, you all go on ahead," said Captain Edwards. "I'll take the chopper up the canyon.  If I see anything, I'll radio back.  Arnie, these men are killers; and they obviously know their way around the park."

The captain didn't have to say anymore.

"I'll be careful, Captain."

Captain Edwards nodded and headed back to the chopper.

"Saddle up," said Logan.

They loaded up their backpacks and headed down the canyon.

__________

Malcolm didn't care what it was.  He ate it until it was gone.  Smith had already loaded Malcolm's bowl twice.  Clarisse had eaten a full bowl herself and then laid down on a mat in the corner of the room.  She was asleep in minutes.  Into his third bowl, Malcolm finally stopped to drink some of the coldest water he'd ever tasted.

"How do you keep the water so cold?"

"Trade secret.  The less you know the better." said Smith.

He thought for a minute.

"Now, I know why they're after her.  How did you get pulled into this?"

Malcolm knew there was something wrong.  No man would live up here in the wild without a serious reason.  It could be of his own volition, but more than likely he was hiding too.  But whatever his reason for being here, he had saved their lives; and a certain amount of trust was warranted.

"My name is Malcolm McBride.  I'm a Detective with the NYPD.  My partner and I were assigned to protect her, but we obviously didn't do a very good job."

"Is your partner okay?"

"I think he got shot.  I'm hopeful that the Calvary got there in time, but I don't know.  I really need to get to a phone.  Will you help me?"

"Let's see if we can get your arm straightened first.  If we don't do something soon, it may be too late to keep you from losing the use of it."

"What do you know about it?" said Malcolm.

"Well, I've had to fix a few broken appendages in my time.  It's all predicated on getting the bone straight.  Let's go outside so we won't wake the child."

Malcolm limped outside, and they went about twenty yards into the woods.

"Okay, lie down on your belly."

Malcolm struggled to get back down, and then laid on his belly facing, Smith.

Smith put both of his feet against Malcolm's shoulders and then reached down and gently took Malcolm's broken arm by the hand.

"Now, I'm going to pull back toward me as hard as I can. When I let your hand go, the bones will be in alignment. You must keep it straight out in front of you. You will want to pull it back to your body. It's a natural reaction. If you do that, you will cause the ends of the bones to move, and we'll have to do it again. Trust me, you don't want to do this but once."

Malcolm took a deep breath.

"Here," said Smith handing Malcolm a piece of pine bark.

Malcolm put it between his teeth.

"Okay, do it!" he said.

Smith pulled his arm slowly holding tightly to Malcolm's hand. When he reached the angle of the break, he said, "Hang on!"

Pulling hard, he brought the arm forward forcing the separated bones to extend fully. Holding the hand and the extended arm for about three seconds, he slowly allowed the arm to move back towards the shoulder. The two ends of the ulna were now aligned. Malcolm did not pull the arm back because he had passed out. Smith quickly checked his breathing and removed the broken pine bark from his mouth. He hadn't made a sound but had bitten the pine bark in to.

Smith put two pieces of kindling from the firewood on both sides of the arm and tied it.  It was crude but effective.  He decided to check his ankle.  It was still badly swollen, but there didn't seem to be any breaks.  He moved the ankle back and forth to break up the blood clots adhering to the ligaments.  Almost immediately, Smith could tell that the range of motion had increased.  It would be sore as hell when he woke up, but he would be able to put weight on it in about three days.  He carefully rolled the big man over on his back and placed some leaves under his head.  Checking Malcolm's breathing again, Smith went back to the cabin.  In a few minutes, he returned with a deer hide, and wrapped Malcolm in it.

"Rest for awhile, Detective.  I've got some thinking to do."

---

The sun began to filter through the trees slowly penetrating the conscious areas of Malcolm's brain.  He opened his eyes.

"You look like a beached whale."

Malcolm squeezed his eyes and briefly tried to raise his arms. The searing pain from the one that was broken brought him back to the reality of where he was.

"Say what?"

"I said you look like a beached whale.  What did Smith wrap around you?"

Clarise had asked what had been done with Malcolm and Smith had pointed outside. With little effort she had found him.

Malcolm looked at the hide and remembered why he was lying on the ground.

"It's a deer hide.  How long have I been here?"

"Since yesterday evening."

"I slept out here all night?"

"Smith said you were too heavy to move and too exhausted. You feel better?"

Malcolm carefully pulled the hide away with his good arm and sat up.

"Yeah, I do.  I'm hungry again."

"He's inside fixing something.  It smells good, so I didn't ask what it was.  He told me to come get you."

With Clarisse's help, he got to his feet; and they walked back to the cabin.  Lying on the table was a cell phone. Malcolm sat down and looked at it.

"I found it a few weeks ago in a backpack.  I don't know what happened to the owner.  Can't imagine that they would just walk off and leave it.  I think there is probably just enough juice left in it to make your call."

Smith brought over his breakfast concoction and dumped it into two bowls.  His two guests never asked; they just dug in like it was the greatest meal they'd ever had.

"I'm going outside to feed, Rage.  Be back in a few minutes."

Malcolm nodded.

"Are you gonna make the call?" said Clarisse.

"In a few minutes," said Malcolm.  "You wait here, I need to talk to Smith."

Smith was sitting on the ground watching Rage tear into his breakfast.

"I never had anything hurt as bad as setting my arm. I've been cut, shot, and clubbed on the head.  Nothing compared to setting a broken arm."

Smith laughed.

"How's your ankle feel?"

Malcolm had walked out with the crutch and had not tested the ankle.  He switched the crutch to the other arm, and gently set his foot on the ground.

"Still hurts, but not as bad.  You work on that too while I was out?"

"Just moved it around a little.  You should be able to walk on it in a couple of days."

Malcolm sat down and began to rub Rage's back.

"There is no way I can possibly repay you for what you've done for Clarisse and me.  We'd be dead if you hadn't come along."

Smith just nodded and rubbed Rage's nose.

"My name is not Dub Smith.  You've probably figured that out."

"I figured," said Malcolm.  "I don't care what it is. You've already shown me who you are.  Whatever you've done in the past makes no difference to me."

"It would make a difference to others."

"Maybe so, but I'm dealing with the here and now.  I've got to get Clarisse back to New York and in protective custody.  Which direction is the ranger station?"

"Just go straight through the woods about a mile, and you'll come on a ridge.  It's steep, but at the bottom is the Appalachian Trail.  Just follow it east, and it will take you right to the station.  I'd say about five miles.  You need to wait a couple of days, so the ankle will heal up."

"You think you can put up with us for that long?"

Smith just smiled.

"I had a daughter just like Clarisse.  She was ten when she died.  My wife died of Ovarian Cancer two years before.  That was a long time ago, but I remember it like it was yesterday."

"I'm sorry," said Malcolm.  "I lost my wife to a murdering psychopath a little over a year ago.  But I still have a daughter and grandson.  I can't imagine losing them too."

Smith stared out into the beauty that surrounded them and then lowered his head.

"When I was a kid, my mom used to say when life hands you a lemon, make lemonade.  I've had a hard time seeing the positive side of that statement. "

Smith got up and went back inside.  Malcolm took a deep breath; and as he watched Smith walk into the cabin, he remembered holding Denise in his arms and watching her life's blood pool on the floor.  He too had had a hard time with the lemons.  Like Smith, he looked at the beauty all around him.  At some point, physical pain nearly always goes away.  But the mental agony brought on by unforeseen circumstances is something completely different.  It hangs in the air like coal dust in a mine suffocating and tearing at the very essence of who you are and sometimes rendering you completely helpless of ever recovering.  Malcolm had watched Smith's eyes as he talked about his wife and daughter.  The pain, the incessant pain, had been there a long time.

He went back inside and picked up the cell phone.  He walked out to an area free of trees and dialed a number.

---

"Did he say where they were?" asked Arnie.

"No, he just said to meet him at the ranger station at the park entrance tomorrow.  Clarisse is alright.  He also said, 'Tell Arnie it's his turn to buy.'"

"Okay, I'm headed back up there."

---

"We've lost their trail.  Raymond searched everything in both directions.  We have no idea where they are or how they got out of the hideout."

Abbott was reporting to Meadows knowing that the failure to find the girl could cost them their lives.  Surprisingly, Meadows didn't sound the least bit upset.  He just told them to come back in.

"We're going back," said Abbott to the others. "Apparently the boss has another strategy."

# CALM BEFORE THE STORM

## CHAPTER TEN

Clarisse hugged Smith and then walked beside Malcolm as they headed into the forest.  When she could see he was able to make it on his own, she headed back to the cabin.  Smith knew that if Malcolm didn't keep his word, there would be cops all over the mountain before sundown.  He and Rage went back inside to eat breakfast.

Malcolm sat in an interrogation room with enough suits to outfit every detective assigned to the two-four.  Most were FBI, but Internal Affairs was there along with Captain Edwards.  They were all having a problem with his account of what had happened the three days he and Clarisse were on the run.

"You twisted your ankle.  You broke your arm.  And for three days a twelve-year-old girl hid both of you.  She then splinted your arm and helped you walk on a bad ankle all the way to a ranger station.  That's your story, and you're sticking to it?"

Agent Butts from the FBI looked at the other suits around the table and then back at Malcolm.

"She also caught some fish from the river, scaled 'em with a sharp rock, started a fire rubbing sticks together, and cooked the fish," said Malcolm.  "You're welcome to go back to the cave, and you'll see that we were there.  So, what exactly are you accusing me of?"

"I really don't know," said Agent Butts.  "I can't imagine why in the world you would make up something that is so ridiculous unless you are trying to protect someone."

Agent Butts watched Malcolm's reaction to his last comment but saw nothing except what he'd seen from the moment Malcolm sat down, a blank stare.

"Okay, let's drop this for now.  Where is Clarisse? We need to put her in a safe place."

"Not happening," said Malcolm.  "The last safe place you put her in almost got us all killed."

"You obviously aren't hearing me," said Agent Butts. "You turn that girl over, or your career as a New York detective ends today."

"You're not gonna touch her."

Agent Butts turned to his right to see Captain Edwards, who was now standing and leaning forward with both hands on the table.

"My detective is right.  You have a leak somewhere, and it's not the first time.  If memory serves me, these same two detectives almost got killed at another one of your "safe houses."  And as to Detective McBride's status with the New York Police Department, the FBI has absolutely no jurisdiction as to who I hire and fire.  Now you go tell your boss that we have assumed responsibility for Clarisse's safety; and she will be produced when, and only when, Jarvis Meadows is captured.  Now, this inquisition is over."

Captain Edwards nodded for Malcolm to leave.  He slowly got up and gingerly made his way out the door.  As he closed the door, it sounded like a volcano exploded inside the room.

Malcolm made his way back into the office area and spied Arnie sitting at his desk.

"Well, I see you still have your gun and shield.  What the hell could they possibly have been so upset about?"

It was another ten minutes before Captain Edwards made it back to the office area.  Malcolm and Arnie were busy at their computers updating paperwork.  He sat down across from Malcolm's desk.

"I don't want to know where she is.  I just want to know that she's safe."

"You have my word, Captain.  I think the phrase is 'she's hidden in plain sight.'  Jarvis won't find her.  We just need to focus on him."

"Fine," said Captain Edwards.  "Get to it!"

As he walked back toward his office, Arnie looked over at Malcolm's computer screen.

"None of my business, but why are you trying to check hospital records?"

Malcolm shook his head and looked around the room. There were probably twenty-five murder cases being worked by ten sets of detectives.  Two had been assigned to Malcolm and Arnie, all of that with Jarvis Meadows thrown on the pile.

"Clarisse and I would be dead if not for the help of a fugitive."

Malcolm had Arnie's full attention.  Arnie pulled his chair over, and Malcolm related the whole story from the hide-out to walking down the mountain to the ranger station.

"You're sure he's killed somebody?" said Arnie.

"No, I'm not sure.  But whatever happened involved his daughter, Betsy.  I'm sure that was her real name, but he told us Dub Smith was his.  And other than my incessant compulsion to tie up loose ends, I'm not sure I should even be looking.  The guy saved our lives for Christ's sake!"

"You said his wife died ten years ago of ovarian cancer?"

"Yeah, but hospital records are confidential.  We'd have to get a court order, and I sure don't want anybody to find out I'm looking and ask why?"

Arnie thought for a few seconds.

"Let's just say we're with the American Cancer Society, and we're gathering statistics on how many women died of ovarian cancer in 2003.  That would have been two years after Nine-Eleven.  We're trying to find out if there was any rise in cancer among women that might have been because of contamination from the destruction of the towers."

"That's the stupidest thing I ever heard of," said Malcolm.

"So is the study of why the Great Northern Woodpecker has left the New York area over the last ten years."

"Where the crap did you hear about that?"

"I just made it up.  You think some paper pusher at a hospital would know my survey was anymore dumb than hunting woodpeckers?"

Malcolm nodded.

"Well, I'm curious, but not enough to keep us from finding Jarvis Meadows.  That's gotta take priority."

"Agreed," said Arnie.  "How many hospitals are we talking about?"

Malcolm handed Arnie the phone book.

"It's gonna take a while."

When Malcolm knocked on Rose Marie Shaffer's door, she never hesitated to do what he asked.  He and Arnie had saved her from a murdering abusive father and all his relatives down in Texas.  She had been fifteen years old at the time.  She was nineteen and in her second year of college at NYU majoring in business.  She still waited tables at a restaurant which the two detectives frequented often to check on her.  The death of Malcolm's wife, Denise, had been a life-changing tragedy for him.  But somehow, he continued to press on; and as far as she was concerned, he was the father she'd never had.

Clarisse Mitchell had been with Rose almost a week.  As Rose moved from table to table, customer, to customer, she glanced through the window into the kitchen.  Big Joe, the owner, had agreed to let Clarisse wash dishes and work in the back of the restaurant.  Being only twelve, she couldn't officially be on the payroll; but money changed hands anyway.  The number one rule was to always stay in the back.  When Malcolm had brought Clarisse over, he said he and Arnie wouldn't be able to drop by the restaurant for awhile but not to worry. They knew she was in good hands.  To Rose, that was all that needed to be said.  Clarisse was in trouble, and Rose had been assigned to protect her.  Growing up in the backwoods of Texas, she knew all about guns; and she would have no problem shooting the first person to threaten Clarisse Mitchell.

Clarisse looked out the serving window and watched Rose wait on the customers.  She had taken an immediate liking to the "country girl".  Because of the hell they had lived in, they both had grown up way too fast.  They had a lot in common.

As soon as the FBI caught Jarvis Meadows and got her testimony, Clarisse was headed for foster care.  Being only twelve years old, it was a certainty.  But that was down the road.  Right now, she had found a friend; and Clarisse intended to do everything in her power to make sure nothing ruined it.

# A MESSAGE IN BLOOD

## CHAPTER ELEVEN

Calvin Dirks made the biggest mistake of his young life. The deadline to pay his debt had passed.  His five-thousand-dollar loan had now escalated to fifteen thousand.  Calvin couldn't pay the five much less the fifteen.  The original five had been borrowed on a sure thing, a horse that couldn't lose.  The payout would have been significant if the horse had won.  But as is often the case on sure things, it was not a sure thing.  Since the loan couldn't be repaid, Calvin would now forfeit his life.  Jarvis Meadows usually let his soldiers take care of trivial matters, but today was different.  As Calvin was being taken away, he made an additional mistake of calling Meadows a gutless coward who let others do his dirty work. Meadows had almost beaten Calvin to death.  That had been two hours ago.  Lying motionless in the back of the van, Calvin was now fully awake and aware that he was being taken somewhere to be killed.  Along with the three in the van, Jarvis was going to use Calvin for target practice.  Calvin had learned all of this by simply listening to the conversations.

"So, what about the Mitchell girl? You heard anything?"

"No one's heard a word," said Nathan.  "One thing we do know.  The FBI doesn't have her."

Meadows turned and looked at the prostrate body of Calvin Dirks.

"Well, they have to capture me before her testimony has any validity.  She'll surface sooner or later.  In the meantime, tell Raymond and Abbott to take Hansboro as soon as he gets home tomorrow."

The conversation soon returned to how accurate their guns would be at fifty to a hundred feet.  With Meadows steadily watching Calvin's motionless form, several bets were made.  Calvin felt the van turn onto a dirt road and slow down.  He opened one eye just as Meadows turned around.

"Well, welcome back to the living."

Calvin pulled his knees up to his chest as far as he could and waited.  With his hands tied behind his back, his options were severely limited.  The truth in fact was he had no options.  The van stopped, and he heard footsteps walking down the side.  The door opened; he was jerked out.  When he landed on his feet, he ran.  He heard laughter as he stumbled and fell to the ground.  He struggled to his knees and was almost on his feet when the first bullet slammed into his right hip.  It turned him completely around, but he managed to stay up and started to run again.  There was so much pain in his hip that he unintentionally began to weave which made the next volley scream through the air exactly where he should have been.  The adrenaline kicked in, and he began to run faster.  He was more than fifty feet away when the next bullet caught him in the back.  The blow caused the air to explode from his lungs as if he'd been shot in the chest.  Somehow in his subconscious he was told to fall meant death, so he continued to stumble forward but lurched violently to his right.  That alone saved him from another volley that missed him by inches.  But this time he was not able to right himself and he fell down the embankment beside the road.  He rolled over and over his body crashing through rocks and brush finally landing at the base of a large boulder over a hundred feet down.

"See him?" said Meadows as he walked over to the side of the road.

"Nothing," said Raymond as he and the others walked up.  "But nobody could have lived through that!"

"Go down there and put a bullet in his head," said Meadows.

"Are you serious?" said Raymond.

Meadows put his gun against Raymond's head.

"Does is look like I'm serious?"

It was after five o'clock.  Enough light to see but not for long.  Raymond started down the hill, and it seemed that with every step he started a small avalanche of gravel and rock.  He was within sight of the body when he spotted a snake coiled and looking right at him.  He quickly looked back up but could see nothing, which meant Meadows couldn't see him either.

He moved a couple of steps closer and fired one shot at the snake.  He missed, but that was okay.  He started back up.

Calvin had watched the whole thing.  With his head sandwiched between two rocks, he shouldn't be conscious much less alive.  But alive he was as the torn and battered parts of his body announced to his brain.  All the ganglia, sensory neurons, and synapses that kept the brain informed of pain were working overtime now.  He'd hit his thumb with a hammer one time, and he thought nothing could ever compare to that.  He was wrong.  With superhuman effort he rolled over on his back.  The bullet that had hit him in the back missed his lung.  Though painful, he could breathe.  He began to slowly flex his fingers and hands.  Again, pain, but tolerable.  Moving his lower body was altogether a different story.  He couldn't move his right hip without crying out.  After waiting for the pain to ease, he rolled slowly over on his left and then back on his stomach.  To stay here meant death for sure.  No one would ever find him, at least not alive.  He reached out with both hands and pulled himself forward.  That's when he discovered his left arm was broken.  He passed out.

---

"Malcolm, I need to see you and Arnie."

Captain Edwards stood at the door to his office motioning them inside.

"I just got a call from Captain Needmire at the three-seven.  A body was discovered by a couple of hikers in an isolated area off Lee Road.  It was a male, around twenty, twenty-five.  He'd been shot.  He had a hand-written note on him.  It was covered in his own blood.  Needmire said the name Meadows was on it along with some other scribbling that they didn't understand.  Since Meadows was high on the list of all Five Boroughs, he was calling everyone.  I need you guys to go over to the ME's office and take a look at it."

"On our way, Captain," said Arnie.

## CHAPTER TWELVE

The three-seven was on the other side of Manhattan. They had barely gone three blocks when another call came in asking for any officers in the Cambridge Street area to respond to a robbery at Bailey's Liquor Store. Cambridge was two blocks away.

When the detectives arrived, another patrol car pulled up. Malcolm jumped out and flashed his shield.

"What have we got?" said Malcolm.

"Got the same call you just got, Detective. I'm Clark, this is Williams."

"McBride and Buckholtz," Malcolm replied.

"You think the suspect is still inside?" said Clark.

"Only one way to find out," said Malcolm. "You got a bullhorn?"

Clark nodded and pointed toward the patrol car. Officer Williams ran over and brought it back. Clark nodded for Malcolm to go ahead.

"This is the NYPD. Is there anyone in the store?"

Janet Nelms sat with her back against the counter her hands covering her face.  Before locking the two employees in the freezer, she told one to dial 911. Now she waited.

Malcolm called again for someone inside to answer.

Janet stood up and walked toward the door.  Her eight-year-old son's water pistol hung by her side.  Because of her drinking, she had lost custody.  Her soon to be ex-husband had painted her as an unfit mother and the judge had agreed. Life for Janet Nelms had come to an end.  She didn't have the courage to do it herself.  She had hoped that the owner of the liquor store would have a gun hidden behind the counter, and he would just shoot her.  He didn't have one.  So, with a water pistol, she herded them all into the freezer and waited for the police to arrive.

As she stood at the door, she could see the patrol cars and the officers hiding behind them.  She counted five cars and at least fifteen officers.  But the one with the bullhorn was not dressed like the others.

Malcolm could see her now.  It was a woman, and very rarely do women rob liquor stores.  It's not that they wouldn't, but some things are just more of a man's crime. This was one of them.

"Ma'am! Can you see me?"

Malcolm raised his head above the car putting both hands in the air.

"Are you nuts, Detective?" said Clark.

Clark looked quickly at Arnie, who just shook his head, indicating that Malcolm was in charge.

"Ma'am, I just want to talk.  Is everyone okay in there?"

"They're getting cold, but they're okay," she said.

"What the hell does that mean?" said Clark.

Ignoring the question, Malcolm stood up where she could see him.  With both hands in the air, he walked around in front of the car and placed his gun on the hood.  Pretty sure of the answer to the next question he asked it anyway.

"Is anyone else in there besides customers or employees?"

"No one else," she said.

Malcolm turned and looked at Arnie.

"I can see her," said Arnie. "If she raises that gun, I'm gonna take her out."

Malcolm nodded.

"Ma'am, I'm Detective McBride.  I'm coming over to the sidewalk.  I mean you no harm.  I just want to see if we can work this out."

"There's nothing to work out, Detective.  If you try and come over here, I'll kill you."

Malcolm took a deep breath and glanced back at Arnie, who nodded.

As he walked across the street, she suddenly appeared in the doorway.  Malcolm looked at the gun and knew immediately it wasn't real.  It was too big, and she was holding it with one hand.  He veered over in front of Arnie's line of sight.  The other two officers also had a clear shot, and both were waiting like Arnie for her to raise the weapon.

Malcolm's senses were immediately focused on why she would have a toy weapon.  It didn't take him long to figure it out.

"My grandson has a plastic gun just like that.  Where did you buy it?"

He had just let the officers know that the gun was not real.  Arnie stood up and walked over to Clark and Williams.

"You did hear that didn't you?" said Arnie.

"You've got to be kidding.  That gun isn't real?" said Williams.

"If my partner says it's a toy, that's what it is.  Just watch and listen."

Malcolm had put one foot on the sidewalk when Janet raised the gun.  What she had fully expected to happen didn't.  Malcolm stopped about ten feet away.

"Ma'am, do you have children?"

His statement surprised her.

"A son," she said.

"How old?" said Malcolm.

"Four years."

Malcolm watched the tear begin to trace its way down her cheek. He now knew something had happened concerning the boy.

"I have a daughter. She's full grown now, but she lost her mother last year. A man killed her."

Janet looked up for the first time to see who stood in front of her.

"You lost your wife?"

"Yes."

"I guess I've taken it a lot harder than she has, but the fact remains that she lost her mother. Is your son living?"

"He's with his father. I'm an alcoholic."

"I seriously considered killing myself when Denise died. But somehow, I pulled through it. I had lots of help, believe me."

"I've got no friends to help me."

"That's not true. My name is Malcolm McBride. What's yours?"

She looked at this massive man standing in front of her, and for some reason she said, "Janet, Janet Nelms."

"I'm your new friend, Janet.  If you'll let me, I'll introduce to another one."

Malcolm turned and motioned for Arnie to come over.

"Bring Clark and Williams."

The street was completely blocked off with at least twenty-five officers all standing and watching.

"Janet, this is my partner, Arnie Buckholtz. "

Arnie immediately reached out and took her hand.

"Glad to meet you, Janet.  This is Officer Williams and Clark."

As awkward as they both felt, they too shook her hand.

Malcolm reached inside his coat and pulled out a card. He began to write on the back of it.

"Janet, this is my office number and my cell.  If you need me for any reason, you don't hesitate to call.  Now Officer Williams and Clark are going to take you over to the hospital to see that you're okay.  I'm going to call some more people who will help you with the alcohol problem.  And before you know it, you'll have more friends."

He placed his hand against the side of her face, and she grabbed it like a drowning person would a life preserver.

"And as soon as I get back to the station, I'll have someone look into the situation with your husband and son."

She nodded and walked toward Clark and Williams, two new friends.

"How in the hell did you know that gun wasn't real?" said Arnie as he watched Janet walk away.

"It was an Uzi.  When was the last time you ran into one of those?"

"You could tell it was an Uzi from way back here?" Arnie indicating a spot about twenty feet away.

"I have this innate God given ability to analyze and interpret certain situations."

They began to walk back toward the car.

"So, let me get this straight.  You can not only anticipate something before it happens, but you're able to predict the outcome?"

"In many instances, yes."

"Okay, I feel compelled to do something right now that has a direct bearing on whether Janet goes to prison or the hospital for the treatment she needs.  In your never-ending God given ability to anticipate the future, what am I about to do?"

Malcolm thought for a few seconds and then smiled.

"You're going to be sure the DA knows that the gun she was using was a toy."

"Nope, Oh Great Swami, that ain't it."

Arnie started walking back toward the liquor store.

"There are three human popsicles in a freezer that desperately need thawing out.  I doubt they'll make it till morning."

# LOGAN HANSBORO

## CHAPTER THIRTEEN

"The ID in his wallet said his name is Calvin Dirks."

The ME looked up just as Malcolm and Arnie walked in. The detectives immediately saw the holes in the hip and back.

"How many times was he shot?" said Malcolm.

"Twice, but that's not what killed him."

The ME showed the detectives the three puncture marks on Dirks' arm, shoulder, and leg.

"He was snake bitten three times.  The venom finally stopped his heart. "

"His fingernails are nearly torn off," said Arnie as he picked up Dirks' right hand.

"Yes, said the ME, "and with a broken left arm he still managed to crawl up a hundred-foot embankment to the road.  Apparently, when he got there, he knew he was dying. He found an empty bag with a straw in it.  Well, you can see what he wrote in his own blood."

Arnie carefully picked up the bag.  In blood, Calvin had written three words: Meadows, Mitchell, and Hansboro  F - 4.

Arnie looked down at Calvin Dirks' body.

"He put up one hell of a fight, didn't he?"

"He sure did," said the ME.  "You got any ideas as to what the names mean?"

"Oh yeah, we know what they mean.  We'll take this with us, Doc," said Arnie.

As they walked back outside, Malcolm kicked a trash can off the sidewalk out into the street and then walked over and leaned against the car.

"Dirks told us who killed him and who Meadows is still after.  Got a clue on what the rest of it means?" said Malcolm.

"Shouldn't be too hard," said Arnie.  "Hansboro is not a common name.  I'm not sure what he meant by F-4, but once we find out who Hansboro is I'll bet the rest of it falls in place."

---

Logan Hansboro walked out of the bank and climbed in his car.  It had been a long day.  Janelle and Christi were patiently waiting for him to get home.  They had a big weekend planned. Being the President and CEO of Chase Manhattan Bank had given him a sixth sense which had now become a part of his psyche.  As he pulled into the driveway, Christy was not waiting on the porch.  Except for her piano lessons which were on Tuesday, she was always waiting for her daddy to get home.  And today they were leaving for the big weekend.  She would have already been out the front door.  The drapes were also drawn.  Janelle never closed them until evening.  He stopped the car and turned off the ignition.

"What's he doing?" said Raymond.

Abbott had been watching behind the drapes.

"Don't know," said Abbott.  "Looks like he's trying to round up some papers."

They watched as Hansboro continued to stay busy in the car not knowing that he had called 911.  As they had been told, the officers answering the call arrived without their sirens.  After nearly ten minutes in the car, Hansboro climbed out and headed up the sidewalk.  He opened the front door already knowing his wife and child were being held hostage.  Immediately, a gun was pressed to his back; and the door slammed.

"Didn't think you were ever coming in," said Raymond.  "What the hell were you doing out there?"

"Making sure my family wasn't harmed," said Hansboro.

"Exactly what does that mean?" said Raymond.  "Search him!"

Abbott quickly ran his hands over Hansboro's body but found nothing.

"I have an offer for you," said Hansboro.

Raymond laughed.

"What offer would that be?"

"Your lives for ours," said Hansboro.  "Look outside."

Abbot quickly pulled back the drapes.

"Cops!" he yelled.

"My proposition is pretty simple.  You free my wife and daughter, and I'll be your hostage.  I will take you to the bank or anywhere else you want to go."

"How about we just kill your wife and kid if the cops don't leave in the next two minutes?" said Raymond.

"You could do that.  And then you'd have to kill me too because I'm not going anywhere if they're harmed."

Abbott laughed.

"He's crazy.  Meadows didn't say anything about this guy being nuts."

Raymond walked over and jerked Christy up by her hair and put the gun in her ear.  You could barely hear Raymond's command to open the door over Janelle's scream.  He walked out the front door using Christy as a shield.

"Who's in charge?" he screamed.

"That would be me," said a big man in plain clothes.

Every station in the Five Boroughs had the name of Hansboro on the "hot list."  As soon as the 911 call came in, it was immediately routed to the two-four.  Malcolm and Arnie were out the door in minutes.

"I want all these cops out of here, or I will kill this girl," said Raymond.

Malcolm walked up to the sidewalk in front of the house.

"You willing to trade your life for hers?"

"You think I won't kill her?" said Raymond.

"No, I believe you will.  I'm just telling you that if you harm anyone in that house, you'll never make it to lockup."

"You must be the cop that shot Meadows.  He described you to us.  Maybe I'll just kill you right now and save Meadows the effort."

Malcolm laughed.

"Okay, we're leaving.  I don't know how you think this is going to end, but we'll play it your way for awhile."

Malcolm walked back to the line of police cars.

"Okay, everybody drive down to the next block and wait."

Within minutes, all the patrol cars had disappeared from the front of the house.

"I should have dropped him right there in the front yard," said Raymond as he watched through the drapes. "Meadows would probably give me a medal."

"More likely he'd have killed you," said Abbott.

"Well, I think I'll take your suggestion and go by the bank.  My partner will stay in the car with your family.  How's that sound?" said Raymond.

Hansboro didn't comment.  He opened the front door and walked out with Janelle in front and Christy in Abbott's arms.

"Get in the car," said Raymond.

He handed Hansboro the keys and pointed for Abbott to put Janelle and Christy in the back.  Hansboro climbed in and adjusted the rearview mirror so he could see Janelle's face.

"Move!" said Raymond.

Hansboro backed the car out of the driveway and started down the street.

"Where to?" he asked.

"Just drive.  I'll tell you when to turn."

Hansboro glanced in the mirror and made eye contact with Janelle.  He also noticed another car pull in behind them about a block away.  Abbott turned and saw it too.

"They're following us," said Abbott.

"You think they wouldn't?" said Raymond.  "They won't try anything.  Turn right at the next corner."

"You actually think they're going to let you go through with your plan?" said Hansboro.

"They will, or somebody in this car is going to get shot and thrown out the door."

Hansboro glanced in the mirror again.  Janelle nodded ever so slightly.  Hansboro increased the speed up to fifty.

"You in a hurry?" laughed Raymond.

Ignoring the question, Hansboro slid his hand around the steering wheel and pushed a small red button attached to the steering column.

Malcolm and Arnie were about a block behind the Lincoln.

"You got any ideas yet?" said Arnie.

"Not yet," said Malcolm.

The words were barely out of his mouth when the roof covering the front seat of the Lincoln exploded, and the passenger seat carrying a man was shot fifty feet in the air.

"What the hell...." said Arnie.

As Raymond was ejected, a bullet proof glass slid up between the front and back seat of the car.  Hansboro pulled the Lincoln over to the side of the road and cut the engine.  Turning, he looked at Abbott through the glass.

"Now, if your buddy's not dead, he's close to it.  There are cops behind us, and I'm sure in front.  You harm my family and by all that's holy, I will kill you myself.  Now hand my wife the gun."

The shock on Abbott's face changed to fear and panic.  He handed Janelle the gun.

Malcolm had braked just in time.  He pulled over to the side and quickly got out of the car.  The man who'd threatened Christy's life was obviously dead strapped in a seat belt still attached to the seat.  His neck was broken so badly his head was almost ripped from his shoulders.  The Lincoln was parked about a half block away.  The detectives saw the doors open.  Hansboro climbed out along with his wife and child, and it appeared the woman was holding a gun on the other kidnapper.  They all began walking back to where Malcolm had parked the car.

Without waiting to be asked, Hansboro handed the gun and Abbott over to Arnie.

"Sometimes being the President and CEO of one of the biggest banks in New York has some unexpected advantages. Janelle and I took an FBI sponsored class on what to do if we were ever kidnapped.  My board of directors then bought me this Lincoln which is bullet proof, body, and glass.  In the eyes of the FBI, if the whole family was taken, the chances were pretty good that I'd be forced to drive; and one of the kidnappers would be sitting in the passenger seat.  The seat ejection device was placed under the passenger seat which had the same power as ejecting a pilot from a jet airplane.  As you can see, it came in pretty handy.  Course none of this would have been worth a crap if we'd been taken in their vehicle."

The two detectives had to laugh.

"You guys gonna be okay?" said Arnie.

"Just fine," said Hansboro.  "We have a big weekend planned.  You detectives mind if we get to it?"

"Be our guest," said Arnie.

———————

Back at the station, they began to fill out the paperwork.  Since the FBI was never called, they were requiring a blow by blow of everything that happened.

"What's Sammy the Slingshot's name?" said Arnie.

Malcolm laughed.

"You mean Raymond Shields?"

"And the other one?" said Arnie.

"Miles Abbott."

Arnie continued to write.

"Abbott will never give up Meadows.  He's too scared."

"Well, we've whittled down his gang some.  I'm sure he'll reload.  But finding someone that will do his bidding and who also has some semblance of a brain won't be easy," said Malcolm.

Another hour went by.  Arnie went into Captain Edward's office to hand in the paperwork.  When he came back out, Malcolm was staring at his monitor.

"What's got your attention?"

Malcolm turned the monitor, so Arnie could see it.

"Someone that looks familiar for some reason."

The face of an ordinary man stared back.  There were no visible scars, nothing to distinguish him from any other white Caucasian male.

"His name is Royce Chambers.  He's a fugitive accused of killing three people in a health clinic ten years ago."

The detectives continued to read the FBI bulletin.  Chambers apparently had become enraged because there was a problem getting his daughter, Betsy, immediate treatment for a serious health problem.  Chambers had killed the admitting nurse and two orderlies that had refused to help her.

Malcolm turned away from the monitor.  Arnie watched as he got up and walked over to the window.

"You think it's him?" said Arnie.

Malcolm didn't answer.  His thoughts were about the traumatic events of his own life, the kidnapping of his daughter, the murder of his wife, the rescue of Rose Marie Shaffer and Clarisse Mitchell.  His mind flashed back to all the times he and Arnie's lives had been saved by someone else or by the grace of God.

"No, it couldn't be him.  The guy that called himself Dub Smith was bigger and had a scar above his right eye."

He glanced down at his watch.

"Let's go home."

———————

Three months passed with no re-appearance of Jarvis Meadows.  Malcolm and Arnie continued to work homicide cases that never seemed to end, but at the same time were not difficult to get a handle on.  There was always an obvious motive and, in most instances, a viable suspect that popped up pretty quick.  Things were going well with Rose Marie and Clarisse, and the detectives had pretty much healed up from their wounds.

"What are you doing?" said Malcolm.

He had been watching Arnie scroll up and down his computer screen.

"Trying to figure out why the insurance company is still requiring money from me."

Turning to face Malcolm, he said, " I was shot in the line of duty.  Isn't Workman's Compensation supposed to pick up the tab for the surgery, re-hab, the meds., everything?"

Malcolm leaned back in his chair.

"Let me tell you a story that will illustrate the incompetence of hospitals.  A guy named Smith goes to the doctor's office to pick up his wife's test results.  The lab technician tells him there has been a mix up.  When the samples from the guy's wife were sent to the lab, another Mrs. Smith's samples were sent also.  Now they don't know which lab results belong to whom.  Both results are bad, but one is really bad.  Course, Mr. Smith wants to know what that means.  The technician tells him one sample tested positive for Alzheimer's, and the other tested positive for AIDS.  He says we don't know which is which.  Course, Mr. Smith wants to know why can't they just retest?  The technician says that normally they can, but the insurance company has refused to do it.  So, Mr. Smith wants to know what to do?  The technician thinks for a few seconds.

"Why don't you just drop her off downtown.  If she finds her way back home, don't sleep with her."

Arnie turned off the computer.

"You know being around you has made me wonder about the meaning of life.  Why couldn't we just live it backwards?  You die first and get that over with.  Then you go live at an old age home.  You get kicked out for being too healthy.  You go collect your pension; then, when you start work, you get a gold watch on the first day.  You work forty years until you're young enough to enjoy your retirement.  You drink alcohol, party, and get ready for high school.  You go to primary school, you become a kid, you play, you have no responsibilities, you become a little baby, you go back, you spend your last nine months floating with luxuries like central heating, spa, room service on tap.  Then you finish off as an orgasm."

Captain Edwards stood at the door to his office listening.  Inwardly, sometimes he wanted to strangle both of 'em; but as he laughed to himself.  He realized that the two best detectives in all of New York were sitting twenty feet away.  Whatever they had to do to relieve the stress and horror of facing evil, was just fine with him.

"Malcolm, I need to see you and Arnie."

# IT BEGINS

## CHAPTER FOURTEEN

Debra Nix waited as the Cessna made another turn and leveled off.

"You sure about this, Ma'am?" said the pilot.

She looked down at the sea of trees and the small thread that represented the Appalachian Trail winding into the horizon.  With all her experience, she knew that the cross winds would very likely cause her to miss her target.  She had no choice.  Spence and Tim were waiting.  If the ransom wasn't paid, they'd be killed.  She turned toward the pilot and nodded.  She opened the door, and he throttled back for just a few seconds.  When he looked back, she was gone.

Along with making sure she positioned herself correctly to pull the ripcord, she couldn't help but think, *"How were they all going to avoid being killed once the ransom was paid?"*

At one thousand feet she pulled the ripcord on the primary chute and immediately knew she was in trouble.  It only partially opened.  She had to jettison the primary chute before she could deploy the second.

"Spencer Lacy and Tim Nix of the Nix and Lacy Construction Company have disappeared.  They operate the biggest construction company in the New York area.  At the construction site there was a note left demanding two million dollars for their release."

Captain Edwards pushed the note across the desk as Malcolm and Arnie sat down.  They knew the FBI handled all kidnapping cases, so there was something else going on.

Captain Edwards looked at Malcolm.

"Whoever wrote the note demanded that you deliver the money."

Malcolm smiled.

"Jarvis Meadows.  You do know those two men are already dead?"

"Maybe, maybe not," said Captain Edwards. "Regardless, I promised the FBI that we would help any way we could."

Captain Edwards folded his hands and leaned forward.

"And there's something else."

The two detectives could tell by the look on his face that it wasn't good.

"Abel Wright owns a small airport rental agency.  He took a woman up this morning who parachuted out over the

Appalachian Trail.  From his description, it fit Debra Nix, Tim Nix's wife.  He's pretty sure she had money in a backpack."

"That would be suicide, Captain," said Arnie.  "Where in the world did she think she was gonna land in a million acres full of trees?"

"You're right about that, Detective.  It couldn't have been worse unless the chute doesn't open."

Malcolm and Arnie both looked quickly at each other and then back to Captain Edwards.

"Abel Wright said he never saw the primary or secondary chutes open."

———————

Royse Chambers followed Rage along the ridge.  It was time for the wolf to find his dinner for the day.  It wouldn't take long.  When he was a pup, Chambers fed him venison, squirrel, or anything else he was able to trap and kill.  Rage was full grown now, and his hunting instincts were not to be denied.  In fact, whatever he brought down was usually dinner for both.  A deer suddenly jumped up.  It had been lying in the tall grass.  As it bolted for the forest, Rage was right on its heels.  In a few minutes, Chambers heard the tell-tale sound of a kill.  He had been running trying to keep the two in sight, but the deer and Rage were too fast.  He finally came up on the death scene just as Rage tore out the deer's throat.  It was a doe, but big and healthy.  Rage waited faithfully for Chambers to haul the doe up on a nearby tree to gut and clean the carcass.  After the innards had been disposed of, except for what Rage ate, Chambers threw the carcass over his shoulder and headed back to the cabin.  It was a beautiful day.  The meat from this doe would be salted and dried to be eaten during the winter when game was not so plentiful.

Rage heard it first.  The sound of a plane engine. Chambers placed the carcass on the ground and looked for a spot where the trees didn't obliterate the sky.  He saw an opening and looked up just as someone jumped out of the plane.  He'd never parachuted himself, but one didn't have to be a rocket scientist to see that something was terribly wrong as the jumper fell toward the earth.  The parachute only partially opened.  A human body would reach speeds of over one hundred sixty miles an hour as it descended; and even with a chute partially opened, it would still be falling at around one hundred.  Stunned, all Chambers could do was watch.  The body disappeared into the trees.  For a few seconds both he and the dog stood there seemingly not knowing what to do.  The pilot would have seen the chute not open and immediately called for someone on the ground to rush to the scene. There was really no reason to try and find the jumper.  No one could have lived through that.  Satisfied that he had rationalized correctly, he went back and picked up the deer carcass and headed back to the cabin.

Two miles away Jarvis Meadows also witnessed the falling body.  He too knew that within an hour park rangers would be scouring the area.  Shaking his head, he stared at the two kidnapped men.

"It seems like I can't catch a break."

Looking at Nix, he said, "Looks like your wife just took a nosedive at five thousand feet with my money."

Nix was too horrified to respond.  Debra had made hundreds of jumps.  He couldn't imagine that anything like this would have happened, and that's why he recommended that the money be delivered this way.  The police would not be involved, and Meadows could take the money and get away.  It never one time entered his mind that not only could his wife have died in the attempt, but that even if she had made the delivery, Meadows had no intention of letting anybody live.

"Get up!" said Meadows.

The two men struggled to their feet.

"Start walking."

He pointed toward the trail.  Both men looked at each other knowing they were about to be killed.

*"At least," thought Nix, "Debra died quickly."*

The tears rolled down his face as he began to remember their lives together and how it all would end.

The two detectives arrived at the park headquarters later that afternoon.  If the chute had not opened, there really was no hurry.  Malcolm had read and reread the note left by Meadows several times.  All it had said was bring two million dollars, which of course, he had no access to.  The note also said he would be contacted.  Park ranger Brad Winthrop introduced himself along with three other rangers, and they all sat down.

"I got your report from the pilot," said Winthrop. "I've had rangers all over that area for the past four hours, but they haven't found anything.  But there is an awful lot of ground to cover.  If she hit the ground, the body will be pretty torn up; and the animal life we have up here will smell the blood quickly.  I doubt if we'll be able to find anything left by the time they get through. "

Winthrop could see that was sickening to the two detectives.  Rangers had been finding human remains along the AT for many years.  If the chute caught in the trees, she might never be found.  Most of these pines ran over one hundred feet and they're side by side covering millions of acres. So, what he had just related was not something new to him.

"Did the pilot give you the coordinates?"

Malcolm nodded and handed Winthrop a piece of paper.

"Well, this will help some; but again, the wind could have blown her miles from where he thinks she went down. You still determined to look even though I've got all available manpower out there?"

"Yes," said Malcolm.

Winthrop walked over to a map and directed the other three rangers to cover certain area north, south, and west.

"I'll cover the east side," said Winthrop.  "You detectives come with me.  We'll cover the area where your pilot says he saw her go down.  We've only got about five hours before dark, so let's get started."

———————

Meadows marched his captives almost a mile before he called a halt.  From his backpack he pulled out some nylon ski rope and began to cut it into pieces.  The two men watched with no understanding.

"If you're gonna kill us, why the rope?" said Lacy.

"I have a friend that I'm sure is on his way by now," said Meadows.  "And I want to be certain that I'm there to welcome him.  In the meantime, I'm gonna let you boys hug these two trees.  If anything happens and I don't get back, I'm pretty sure something out here will find you."

He tied them both securely to the trees and walked back toward the trail.

Meadows knew that Malcolm would be coming soon if he wasn't already in the park.  He dialed 911 on his disposable cell phone and waited.

"What is your emergency, Sir?" said the dispatcher.

"I desperately need to get a hold of a Detective Malcolm McBride of the two-four.  My name is Jarvis Meadows."

"What is the nature of your emergency?"

"Someone has placed a bomb under his car."

He could hear the dispatcher immediately put him on hold.  He knew she was asking a supervisor what she should do.  In a few seconds, a different voice came on the line.

"Mr. Meadows, how do you know this?"

"Because I placed it there.  Now if you don't patch me through to his phone, you're going to have a dead cop on your hands."

Again, the line was put on hold.  It was nearly a minute before Meadows heard the voice that he wanted to hear.

"Jarvis Meadows.  So, what's this about a bomb under my car?"

"Not to worry, Detective.  I wouldn't be so cowardly as to take you out like that.  I want to see your face when you die, like what you thought you saw in mine the last time we met.  Any luck finding Mrs. Nix?"

"So, you set all this up?  Pretty impressive.  I assume you still have her husband and Lacy?"

"Sorta.  Depends on how quick the bears find 'em."

Malcolm squeezed the phone so hard it was a miracle it didn't shatter in his hand.  Winthrop and Arnie both stood stunned.  How had this animal gotten Malcolm's number and what did he want?  Seeing their anxiety, Malcolm switched the phone on speaker.

"Alright," said Malcolm.  "What do you want?"

"Not so fast, Detective.  Whatever happened to the Mitchell girl?  And how did you ever manage to avoid being found?"

"Well, first Clarisse is waiting patiently to testify at your trial which, of course, is never going to happen because I'm going to kill you.  And as to avoiding your intelligent employees, it really wasn't as difficult as it might have seemed.  By the way, how did you ever survive three hollow point bullets to the chest and a fifty foot fall off an ocean cliff?"

"Kevlar, Detective.  Needless to say, it still hurt like hell.  Even with broken ribs, I'm still a better swimmer than most people."

"Kevlar.  I'll have to remember that the next time we meet.  Are you having problems operating without Raymond and Abbott?"

"So, you were part of that too.  I'll have to say this for you.  You do get around.  I would like to continue this conversation, but I need to go check on the meals I left for the bears.  Before you get off the mountain, I'll get another message to you.  And while I'm thinking about it, you need to tell that ranger with you, he needs to have that uniform pressed."

All three dropped to the ground just as a bullet slammed into the tree where Winthrop's head had been two seconds earlier.

"The son of a bitch is looking right at us," said Winthrop.

Malcolm crawled to a tree and stood up behind it.

"He didn't mean to kill you," said Malcolm.  "If he wanted you dead, he could have killed you while we were talking on the phone.  He just wanted to let us know he could take us out anytime he wanted to."

"He convinced me," said Winthrop.

Winthrop's radio began to buzz indicating that the other rangers had heard the shot.  Winthrop quickly assured them that he was fine.  Looking over at Malcolm, he asked, "Do I need to bring them in?"

Malcolm nodded.

"I don't know what he plans, but we can't take a chance on him killing more people.  Tell 'em to come back."

Meadows continued to watch the three through the scope.  It would have been no challenge to kill all three, but that would have activated the National Guard.  He didn't want that many people at the party.

# NOT ALONE ANYMORE

## CHAPTER FIFTEEN

Chambers and Rage got back to the cabin close to dark. He laid the deer carcass on the steps and began to cut it up. Some he would salt and let dry. Some of the other he would wrap and put in the creek. The temperature was just above freezing, so the meat would keep for awhile. The rest he would make into stew. In a few minutes, Rage became restless and trotted off into the forest. Chambers never worried. Whatever danger the wolf might find, he was more than capable of holding his own. Several hours passed before he reappeared. Chambers was sitting on the porch and watched the big wolf dragging something. As he approached the porch, Chambers could see it was a backpack.

"What have you got, Boy?"

The backpack was ripped and torn on the outside, but the damage had still not resulted in the inside of the bag being exposed. Chambers pulled on the zipper.

He didn't count the money. It had to have belonged to the jumper. And if the jumper had that kind of money, something else was going on. He and Rage started back into the forest. At night, the forest was claustrophobic. Only ten years of living in the wild kept him from falling into ravines or stepping on sleeping carnivores. Even still, he knew that roaming in the forest was tantamount to suicide.  Still, with Rage running point, he made his way back to the area that he knew had to hold the remains of the jumper.  After nearly twenty minutes, the wolf stopped indicating something was ahead.  Chambers stopped and knelt.  He could hear footsteps about a hundred yards away.  As they began to recede, Rage continued for another few minutes but suddenly stopped again.  There was a loud noise of something coming through the woods.  Chambers had heard animals prowl before and knew it was big.  Soon, he heard another sound, but this time human.  It sounded like someone chanting or praying.  Chambers approached carefully and saw two men bound to trees.  One was slack against the ropes, and the other was praying.  Rage went on ahead and sat at the feet of the one in prayer.  For a few seconds, the man didn't see the wolf; and then he did.

"He won't harm you," said Chambers.

The terrified man looked frantically around until he found the owner of the voice.

"Who are you?" he said.

"Looks like I'm your savior.  What's your name?"

"Tim Nix."

"Please, check on my son!"

Chambers looked over and saw a boy slumped down against the ropes.

"Is he okay?" said Nix.

Chambers walked over and raised the boy's head.

"I think he's fainted."

He gently lowered his head back down.  With a knife, he cut the boy's bindings and laid him on the ground.

"What's his name?"

"Spencer Lacy. We were kidnapped and left out here to die."

"Well, that wouldn't have taken too much longer."

Chambers untied Nix and then knelt to check on Lacy again.  With a canteen and cloth, he began to bathe Lacy's forehead.

"I think he'll be alright in a few minutes.  Go back down this trail about three miles, and you'll find the ranger station."

"You're not gonna leave us, are you?" said Nix.

"Yeah, you'll be alright."

Chambers began to walk away.

"But what's your name?" yelled Nix at the retreating figure.

In a few seconds, Rage and Chambers were gone.  In another twenty minutes, they had arrived at what Chambers felt was the drop zone.  For the first time, he opened a bag and took out a flashlight that he'd also found in a lost backpack. He'd only tested it once, but it had worked then. It worked now as he slowly began to survey his surroundings. The foliage was as dense as it had been since the beginning of time. He flashed up above him and saw nothing. With Rage leading the way, they walked in a large circle again carefully checking and rechecking the area for anything dangerous. They had almost given up when Rage stopped near a tree. There were signs of something being dragged from the tree back towards where Chambers was now standing. As he flashed his light around, he spotted the broken weeds and grass where Rage had dragged the backpack. Chambers walked up to the tree and began to look around. There was nothing. He began to search the surrounding trees carefully walking back and forth with the flashlight beam combing everything within twenty yards of where he stood. He was about to give up when he walked right into a strand of nylon cord. Quickly, looking up, he saw the chute wedged between two large branches. There was a knot on the side of the tree which afforded him a foothold, so he began to climb. Holding with both hands, he found another foothold and pulled himself up again. There was a small notch in the tree where two large branches attached to the main trunk. He sat down and pulled the flashlight out of his pants pocket. He could see the body now. Clothed in black, the body was lying across two large limbs. Putting the flashlight back in his pocket, he reached out and grabbed one arm and pulled the body across the limbs and up against his chest. There was no way he could climb down and hold the body.  Whoever it was wouldn't feel it, but he was reluctant to just drop it to the ground.  He pulled the upper half around until he could see the face.  The helmet and shield still covered it.  The helmet was cracked on one side, and the shield was broken in two places.  He carefully removed both and pushed back the parka.  It was a woman.  Betsy, and his wife flashed through his mind, and he determined he was not going to just drop her to the ground. Shifting her from one shoulder to the other, it took a seemingly endless amount of time. He almost fell twice getting her down.  He was exhausted.  Rage came up and began sniffing all over the body.

"Don't do that, Boy.  I've got to get enough energy to bury her.  It would help if you could find some rocks."

Rage ignored the request and continued to explore the remains.  Satisfied that the lower part provided no interest, he started sniffing and licking the upper.  Chambers finally decided to ignore it and began to look around for a depression or hole in which the body could be placed.  Pulling out his flashlight, he began to search the area and spotted a place where water had run off creating a shallow ditch.  He walked back and picked up the body and gently laid it down. He began to cover it with weeds, twigs, dirt, anything he could find.  He was just about to put a cloth over her face when Rage decided he had to lick her one more time.  He began licking the dead woman's face, and she moaned.

Meadows had just settled down in his one-man tent when he saw the light.  Not knowing whether it was trouble, he decided he'd better explore.  When he got to the location, he saw footprints of both a man and a large dog of some kind.

"Now I wonder who the hell this is?" he said.

He began to follow what he could see now was something being dragged.  There were deep indentations about two feet apart, and the footprints became more pronounced.  Even with no light, he could see the direction the man was headed.  The longer he followed the trail, the more he began to realize that someone lived up here.  The Appalachian Trail would be a great place to hide with thousands of acres in which to disappear.  The detective and Mitchell's miracle disappearance didn't seem so miraculous now.  It was slow going without a light, and it was almost an hour before Meadows walked out of the trees and spotted the cabin.  Not knowing whether the man was armed or the danger of the dog, he decided to go back and get some sleep.

————————

Malcolm and Arnie waited at the ranger station. Malcolm felt certain Meadows wouldn't wait long. Maybe by morning it would all come to a head.  He looked across the room at Arnie knowing he was upset.

Arnie could not understand why Malcolm was not sharing information that he knew was being held back.  A fugitive was hiding up in these mountains, a man that

Malcolm had decided was going to stay free.  If in the hunt for Meadows, Royse Chambers was discovered, he would have to be arrested.

Malcolm mourned for the people that Chambers had killed, but had he not made up for that?  After all these years, was there no forgiveness for an obvious wrong that had been done to his child?  To share any of this with Arnie would require that Arnie keep it a secret too.  Malcolm just would not put his best friend into a situation that, if found out, would not only cost him his job but could send him to prison as well.

"We spending the night here?" said Arnie.

Malcolm nodded and walked over to look out the window.  In a few seconds, he turned.

"Arnie I'm ...."

Suddenly, the door burst open.  Tim Nix and Spencer Lacy staggered into the room dehydrated and dying of thirst.

In ten minutes, cold sandwiches and water were being devoured as if it were the greatest meal ever eaten.  The detectives patiently watched knowing the trauma the two men had faced.  As the eating slowed down, Malcolm walked over and sat down.

Looking at Nix he said, "I know this has been hard. Especially since your wife has been reported missing."

Malcolm knew that referring to her as being dead would only make the interview harder.

"Do you have any idea where Meadows might be?"

Nix looked up with tears in his eyes and shook his head.

"I know Debra had promised him she would get him the money without police interference.  It was my idea that she parachute in.  She's jumped hundreds of times, she...."

He couldn't talk anymore, and Arnie gently put a hand on his shoulder.

"Can you tell me anything about the man who helped you escape?" said Arnie.

As Lacy began to describe their rescuer, Malcolm walked over to the window again.  As soon as Lacy mentioned the giant dog, Malcolm knew who it was but kept his back turned.

"He cut you loose and then just walked away?" said Arnie.

Lacy nodded.

Arnie looked over at Malcolm who continued to stare out the window.

Ever since Malcolm and Clarisse had miraculously escaped the fire and Meadow's men, Arnie knew that Malcolm had held something back.  To Arnie, it was clear that it had something to do with this mystery man that had suddenly appeared out of the forest.  He had saved Lacy and Nix from certain death. Was it likely that he had done the same for Malcolm and Clarisse?

"You guys need to get some rest," said Arnie.  "We'll make sure you get back home tomorrow."

"I'm not leaving without Debra," said Nix.

Winthrop, who had been watching and listening, walked over, and sat down.  He had been letting the detectives do their thing, but it was obvious that Nix needed to face the reality of his wife's death.

"Mr. Nix, I had twelve park rangers out all afternoon.  I will send them out again tomorrow.  If need be, I'll ask the Governor to lend me some members of the National Guard. But you need to come to grips with the fact that the chances that she lived through that kind of a fall...."

He didn't finish the sentence.  Nix was sobbing having laid his head down on the table.  Malcolm walked back over and placed a hand on the man's shoulder.

"Come on Mr. Nix.  We'll help you look again tomorrow. There's nothing more we can do tonight."

Nix and Lacy were escorted down the hallway to bedrooms reserved for the rangers.  Malcolm and Arnie sat back down.  It was almost midnight.

"You can't keep protecting this guy, Malcolm."

Malcolm looked up and shook his head.

"I don't know what you're talking about!"

"It's the same guy you found on the computer isn't it? Malcolm, he killed three people!"

"Leave it alone, Arnie!  This is my call!  There are circumstances here that you know nothing about!"

Arnie could see how emotional this had become.  If there ever was a man who knew the difference between right and wrong, it was Malcolm.  Through the years they had both pushed the envelope to the edge.  Fighting evil was always gut wrenching and at times even mind altering.  But a line had been crossed this time.  The people that had died needed justice, and it made no difference what caused their deaths.

"I know that it must have been this man that saved you and Clarisse.  I also know that his killing of these three people was justified in his own mind.  I can't even imagine the horror of what must have caused it."

"No, you can't!" screamed Malcolm.  "You've never lost someone that you loved.  The light in my soul died when Denise died.  I still wake up at night seeing her in my arms covered in blood, and all I can think of is digging up Miguel Rojas and tearing him into so many pieces that the vultures couldn't find them.  This man watched his daughter die in his arms because the sons of bitches tried to make him fill out paperwork before they'd allow her to be treated.  I would have killed 'em too!"

Arnie stood in shock.  The look on Malcolm's face was not human.  He looked like a wild animal.  Arnie walked over to the opposite side of the room and sat down on a sofa.  Clasping his hands, he began to stare down at the floor.  In all the years of working together, they had never said a word in anger to each other.  Malcolm continued pacing the floor opening and closing his fists every muscle in his body rigid.  Finally, he stopped and walked over sitting down in a chair opposite Arnie.

"I can't let this go, Arnie.  I just can't.  He saved my life.  He saved Nix and Lacy's lives.  He saved the life of a twelve-year-old girl that you and I were sworn to protect.  That's got to count for something.  If he goes back, he'll spend the rest of his life in prison.  I just can't do it."

Malcolm walked across the room and went outside.  In a few seconds, Arnie saw him disappear into the night.

# A WHITE KNIGHT

## CHAPTER SIXTEEN

Chambers gently rolled Debra onto her back.  He needed something hard and straight in order to find the broken bones, so he had laid her on the cabin floor.  Starting with her head, he could see a large bruise on the side of her face.  He ran his fingers through her hair and across the skull but didn't find any abnormalities, no cracks or depressions, and no large bumps.  He opened her eyes one at a time and examined them with his flashlight.  The pupils were dilated which was not a good sign.  But there was no blood in her nose or ears, so the concussion might not be severe.  Reluctantly, he began to remove her clothes.  There was no way to assess the damage without it.  In a few minutes, she lay naked; but he covered her up as best he could.  Her neck was not broken.  That in itself was a miracle.  He ran his fingers down the base of her neck and placed her head back down.  He couldn't be sure about her spine; but if she'd broken her back, he doubted if she could have lived lying across tree branches.  Her shoulders seemed to be okay, but the humerus that attached to the left shoulder was broken.  It had almost come through the skin.  He could see the tip of the broken end pressing againt it.  He could also see redness against that side of her chest.  He carefully ran his fingers below her left breast and counted three broken ribs.  Moving to the other side, he found the lower two bones in her right arm were broken, but the ribs were okay.  The flesh between the breasts was bruised badly, indicating the sternum was injured but not broken.  That was a relief.  If she had broken that, she would have suffocated since the rib cage would have been pulled apart probably puncturing the lungs.  She continued to breathe raggedly which was an indication of her brain dealing with a lot of pain.  He had nothing to give her; but she had fought for her life this long, maybe she could fight it through.  Both hips seemed to still be jointed, but the shin bone in the front of her left leg was broken.  It too was almost sticking through the flesh.  It was obvious now that she had hit the top of the trees on her left side.  There was no discoloration in her abdomen, another good sign.  Hopefully, there was little internal bleeding.  Anything like that would kill her, and he could do nothing to stop it.  The other hip and leg looked okay.  There was serious bruising but no visible damage.  Rage, at his guard post, had watched all of this from the doorway.  Chambers went outside and grabbed some kindling to use for splints.  It took nearly an hour to pull bones back in their correct positions, brace them, and bind them. He took some of his shirts, such as he had left from his previous life, and bound them around her chest holding the ribs in place.  She was still unconscious.  If she woke up, and that was a big if, he didn't know if she'd be able to stand the pain.  It took him another twenty minutes to get one of his shirts and a pair of boxer shorts on her.  And now the real problem presented itself.  He inched her back on the travois and placed the end with her head up on the bed.  With his foot, he dragged the only chair in the cabin over to support the bottom half of the travois.  With his arms under her shoulders, he eased her across the grass matting that he used for a mattress.  She began moaning, and he knew he had hurt something.  It couldn't be helped.  She couldn't stay on the cold floor.  After covering her with deer hide, he walked out on the front porch and sat down with Rage.

"I remember when it used to be quiet and peaceful.  Just you, me, and the woods.  Now every time I turn around, I'm being called on to save somebody's butt.  We're gonna get found, Partner.  And when we do, you're going back to the wild and I'm...."

He didn't finish.  He heard Debra moan, and he walked back into the cabin.

# AN ANGUISHED DECISION

## CHAPTER SEVENTEEN

Malcolm had walked aimlessly up and down the trail for nearly an hour before he realized he was headed to the cabin. He hadn't meant to go.  He was so confused and hurt over Arnie's unreasonable .... Arnie was not being unreasonable. He was thinking logically which Malcolm had refused to do.  It was just a matter of time before someone else stumbled on Chambers.  The park rangers were all over the place.  It was a miracle that the cabin hadn't been spotted before now.  Some things are never black and white.  A person is murdered. The person responsible pays for it.  It's cut and dried, isn't it?  He walked out of the woods and spotted the cabin.  Rage was immediately alerted and sprinted toward the invader of their precious space.  Chambers had spotted the big man almost as soon as he cleared the woods.

"Kinda late for a social call, Detective."

Malcolm knelt and let Rage smell.  In seconds, the big wolf remembered and jumped-up allowing Malcolm to wrap his arms around him.

"Yeah, it is."

"I don't have anything to offer you but cold water."

"That'll be fine."

Chambers walked back into the cabin and brought out a pitcher and cup.  They sat down on the porch.

"So, since this ain't social, are you here in an official capacity?"

"I don't know what I am, Royse."

It was the first time that Malcolm had ever called Chambers by his first name. Chambers glanced at the big man's face and could see he was in the depths of an emotional struggle.

"Those two guys find their way back to the station?"

"Yeah."

Malcolm looked off in the woods and watched Rage chase some invisible critter.

"You keeping count of the people you save?" said Malcolm.

"Haven't really thought too much about it."

"A lot of people would be dead right now if you were in prison."

"Maybe so.  And maybe a frog wouldn't bump his butt if he had wings."

Malcolm looked around, and Chambers had a big smile on his face.  They both burst out laughing at the same time.

"Where did you come up with that crap?" said Malcolm.

"Don't know, it seemed appropriate for the depressed mood you seem to be in."

"What do you want me to do, Malcolm?"

"I want you to live as a free man.  I want you to walk off this mountain and go back to the life you had before you lost your wife and child.  And I know that's not possible.  For you it means prison; for me it means a life of regret for bringing you in on top of more damage to my soul which is operating on life support right now."

"I'm not going back.  I have no reason to live as it is. And if I'm locked up...."

Malcolm nodded.

"Would you do me a favor?" said Chambers.

"Whatever is in my power."

"When they come, would you promise me that you'll release Rage back to the wild?"

With tears in his eyes, Malcolm said, "You have my word."

"Come inside, we've got another problem."

It was almost dawn.  Meadows had already moved up
the mountain high enough to see the ranger station.  The
structure was surrounded by glass, so it was easy for
Meadows to see the inside through the rifle scope.  There
were several already seated around a large table eating
breakfast, including Tim Nix and Spencer Lacy.  He lowered
the scope and considered what that new development meant.
Somebody found them, and it wasn't the rangers or the
detectives.  He picked up his scope and looked again.  The
small detective was visible but not Malcolm.  He continued to
search the main living area, but the big man was not
anywhere in sight.  Meadows lowered the scope and thought
for a few seconds.

*"So, if he's not at the station, where would he be?"*

He continued to turn it over and over in his mind.  A
cabin in the woods, the hostages freed, Malcolm and the girl
somehow rescued; it all began to add up.  The twin tracks of
something being dragged through the woods.  Suddenly,
Meadows knew it was a travois.  The mystery man had found
something or somebody.  Meadows smiled and threw the rifle
over his shoulder.

# ANNIE OAKLEY AND CLAMITY JANE

## CHAPTER EIGHTEEN

Clarisse and Rose had just gotten up and were eating breakfast.

"You do realize that they haven't stopped by the restaurant in nearly two weeks," said Clarisse.

"They have cases to work," said Rose.  "They can't come by on a regular schedule."

"I don't like it," said Clarisse.  "Malcolm's cell phone goes straight to voice mail, and Arnie won't tell me anything. I'm calling Arnie again."

She dialed the number, and it rang five times before Arnie finally answered.

"Arnie, where's Malcolm?"

"He can't come to the phone right now, Clarisse.  And you've got to quit calling us during working hours.  Is something wrong?  Are you and Rose okay?"

"We're fine, but you're not telling me the truth.  Where is Malcolm?"

Arnie was just as worried as Clarisse.  When Malcolm didn't come back from his midnight stroll, Arnie had gone looking.  By two o'clock it was evident that he wasn't coming back, but there was nothing that could be done until morning. Well, it was morning.  Arnie decided it would be better to just tell her that he was temporarily missing and that he would update her throughout the day.

"Clarisse, Malcolm walked off last night and didn't come back.  I'm pretty sure he's found something that warrants his attention and just has not checked back in."

"Where are you guys?" she said.

"We're up at the ranger station."

"Have you seen Meadows up there?"

"Yes, but don't worry...."

Arnie heard the click of the disconnect on the other end.  Clarisse had hung up.

"Malcolm's in trouble!  I've got to get to the mountain!"

Rose knew all about the mystery man known as Dub Smith. Through the months they'd lived together, Clarisse had become her best friend.

"You're not going by yourself.  I'm coming too!"

———————

Malcolm stood and looked down at the rise and fall of Debra Nix's chest.  As he looked at Chambers, who was kneeling rubbing Rage's neck, he came to a decision.  God had placed Royse Chambers on this earth to save lives.  There was no other answer for what was happening.  Nobody could be at the right place and at the right time this often.

"She needs a doctor," said Malcolm.

"I know," said Chambers.

"You better get back down to the ranger station and call for a helicopter."

"What would you have done if I hadn't showed up?"

"Waited a few days and hope she got strong enough for me to load her back up on the travois.  I would have gotten her down to the ranger station."

Suddenly, Rage whirled around and headed out the door.  Malcolm and Chambers both looked but saw nothing.  Rage was almost to the forest when a figure rose from the grass with a rifle.

"Call him back," screamed Meadows.  "Call him back, or he's dead!"

Chambers simply yelled, "No, Rage!" And the big wolf stopped in his tracks and began to eye the intruder.

With the gun still leveled at the wolf, Meadows yelled for Malcolm to throw his gun out on the ground.

Meadows began to walk slowly up toward the cabin, his eyes and the gun never leaving the wolf.

"If I find another weapon when I get up there, I'll kill this animal."

"There are no other weapons," said Malcolm.

"Chain him up," said Meadows pointing to the wolf.

"I don't have to do that.  He'll mind.  Just come in and close the door."

Now of all times, Malcolm wished he had an ankle gun like Arnie.

"Well, well," said Meadows as he looked at the body lying in the bed.  "Looks like Mrs. Nix made it after all.  She busted up pretty bad?"

"Pretty bad," said Chambers.

"So, where's the money?"

"There was no money," said Chambers.  "When I found her, she was hanging in a tree almost stripped.  If she had money, it fell somewhere else."

Meadows looked around the one room cabin.

"Well, there's only one way to know if you're lying."

He opened the door to see Rage faithfully sitting on the porch.  Meadows raised the rifle.

"No, please.  I can take you back to where I found her. The satchel or backpack had to be on her back, so it can't be far."

Meadows laughed and lowered the gun.

"So, what are we waiting for?" he said.

"What about Mrs. Nix?" said Malcolm.

"What about her?" said Meadows.  "If she's a problem, I can take care of that."

He walked over and put the muzzle of the rifle against her head.

"Don't do that," said Malcolm.  "We're ready."

As they walked outside, Meadows pointed at the wolf.

"Don't forget what I said about him.  I'll kill him just as sure as I plan on killing this guy," pointing at Malcolm.

"Why not get that over with now?" said Malcolm.

"Patience big man.  When the time comes, I want to enjoy it."

––––––––––––

Rose and Clarisse had no intention of calling anyone. Clarisse knew that Malcolm and she were the only ones that knew of Dub Smith's existence.  By now, Malcolm probably knew Dub Smith's real name; but that didn't change the fact

Smith was a wanted man. So, was Jarvis Meadows.  If Meadows had found Malcolm, maybe; and it was a big maybe, Smith was aware of it.  If he wasn't, he soon would be because Clarisse needed his help.  Rose had determined to follow Clarisse's lead not knowing all the particulars.  If Malcolm was in danger, that was all she needed to know.  They parked the car in the woods about a mile from the ranger station.  They wore caps and sunglasses to hide as much of their faces as possible. Clarise knew that if Malcolm had not been found, he had to be at the cabin.

"Where are we going?" said Rose, as she opened the trunk of the car.

"I think I know where Malcolm might be," said Clarise.

Rose pulled a fully loaded twelve-gauge shotgun from the trunk.

"Okay, I'm right behind you."

Clarisse began to run up and down trails that were almost impossible to see.  She climbed across rocks so fast Rose couldn't keep up and carry the gun too.  Clarisse sensed it and began to slow down.  It took almost an hour to reach the forest area and another thirty minutes to get through it.  When Clarisse broke through and into the opening, she saw the cabin sitting just as she remembered.  She knelt and waited for Rose.

"Is he there?" said Rose.

"I don't know," said Clarisse.  "I don't see Rage.  Come on."

They began to approach the cabin carefully noting that the front door was standing open.

"Mr. Smith?" Clarisse called.

There was no answer, so she climbed up on the porch and peeked inside.  There was a woman on the bed staring back.  The two girls walked inside.

"Who are you?" said Clarisse.

Debra swallowed but couldn't speak.  It was obvious that she was trying, but nothing came out.  Clarisse knelt beside the bed.

"My name is Clarisse Mitchell.  I'm trying to find the man that owns this cabin, Dub Smith.  Do you know where he is?"

Again, Debra tried to talk but couldn't.

"Maybe she needs water," said Rose.  "Ma'am, would you like some water?"

Debra nodded.

Rose found the water jug and cup.  Gently holding her head, she got a cup of water into the dehydrated woman.

"Thank you," she gasped.  "I don't know who you're talking about."

Clarisse turned to Rose.

"I've got to look for him.  If Jarvis Meadows finds Malcolm...."

There was a horrible moan from Debra which made both girls turn.

"Meadows kidnapped my husband and his partner."

She began to struggle to get up.  Rose quickly put a hand on her shoulder to keep her down.  Clarisse knelt back down.

"Meadows killed my mother and father.  The man that lives in this cabin must be trying to help you.  His name is Dub Smith.  Another man, a New York Detective named Malcolm McBride, is searching for Meadows right now."

"I must have been unconscious. I don't remember seeing either one."

Clarisse looked at the splints and knew that Debra was hurt badly.  Smith would have never left her alone. Something or someone had to have come along and forced him to leave.

"Ma'am, I've got to go look for Dub and Malcolm.  Rose will stay here with you."

Rose shook her head and pointed to the door.  Clarisse followed her outside.

"I grew up in the wilderness.  I was taught to shoot a gun and track game before I was ten.  You'll never find 'em.  All you'll do is get lost, and we'll end up hunting you too.  I've got as much riding on this as you do.  Malcolm saved my life too."

Clarisse tried to argue, but it was no use.  She knew Rose was right.

"You'll call me the minute you find anything?"

"Count on it."

They hugged each other and Rose began to walk around the cabin looking for sign.  She spotted three sets of footprints headed toward the forest.

---

Malcolm and Chambers both knew the money was at the cabin.  Malcolm had figured that out knowing Chambers was desperately trying to buy time.  As soon as Meadows got the money, they were both dead.  Chambers had caught Malcolm's eye several times with that same questioning look.  Malcolm's arm was barely out of the cast, and his ankle still bothered him.  He wasn't sure he was physically able to do anything if and when the time came.  Although they traveled faster in the daylight, Chambers had tried to take a longer route, but Meadows could see the ruts made by the travois the night before.  To try and stray away from it would only have tipped Meadows that the money was not at the site.

Rose had no trouble finding and following the trail.  As she ran through the woods, she tried to decide what to do when she caught up.  Somehow, she had to get Meadows separated from the others.  A twelve-gauge shotgun had a big spray pattern.  It was almost an hour before she spotted them.  The wolf that Clarisse had mentioned was with them.  She couldn't risk getting closer from this angle.  She tested the wind like she'd been taught as a child and began to move down wind of the wolf.


"This is where I found her," said Chambers.  "You can still see most of the chute is still up there."

Meadows glanced up.  He could see the white silk wrapped around some tree limbs.

"You've got ten minutes.  If you don't find it, I'm going to kill you and your animal."

"I'll help," said Malcolm.

"Stay where you are!" said Meadows.

Chambers looked at Malcolm who returned his questioning eyes with a small shaking of the head.  Malcolm was not going to let Chambers die alone.  Walking in a slow circle, Chambers began to create a search pattern widening his circle each time he came back to the starting point.  Malcolm stood helplessly and watched not knowing of anything that he could do except commit suicide against a loaded gun.  Suddenly, about twenty yards away, he saw a head pop up and then just as quick, disappear.  He glanced quickly at Meadows, who was intently watching Chambers.  Each time Chambers knelt to check the ground the head popped up only closer.  The third time he saw it was Rose.  She now stood behind a tree, and he could see the shotgun muzzle.  He turned toward Meadows and yelled out, "One!"

Meadows jerked the gun around and aimed it at Malcolm.

"Two!"

"Shut up, asshole!" screamed Meadows.

"Three!"

And Malcolm dropped to the ground hoping that Rose understood why he was counting.  She did.  The shotgun blast echoed for miles.  Meadow's body was slammed against a tree and then disappeared into the underbrush.  Malcolm raced over and grabbed the gun left lying on the ground.  He raced to the spot where the body should have been, but it wasn't there.  Chambers came rushing over.

"What happened?" he said.

Rose came out from behind the tree.

"Did I get him?" she asked.

Malcolm pulled her into his arms.

"You got him, but he's gone."

They walked over and looked at the ground.  There was blood everywhere.

"He's hit and hit bad," said Malcolm.  "Royse this is a friend of mine.  I'll fill you in on the details later."

With the shotgun in hand, Malcolm began to run back toward the cabin.  In a few minutes, he called for Rose to take the lead.

"Wilderness woman," Malcolm called back over his shoulder to Chambers in an attempt to explain what had just happened.

Meadows was badly hurt, but not so much that he couldn't run.  When Malcolm started counting the numbers: one, two, three were always followed by something.  If his brain had not kicked in at the last split second, he would have caught the full blast in the chest.  He had barely begun to turn on three.  That simple move had saved his life.  He had no idea who the shooter was, but the money was at the cabin. He knew he could find his way out and to a doctor, but he had to have the money.  Nobody was at the cabin but a comatose woman.  Running on pure adrenaline, he was making good time totally unaware of how much blood he was losing.

Rage was running right beside Chambers.  Being a wolf, his instincts told him something was not right; but up to this point his master had not indicated anything that warranted a concern.  Chambers also had not even thought of the lethal weapon that was running beside him.  As they followed the blood trail, Malcolm realized that they would not get back before Meadows.  Even if he didn't survive his wounds, he would kill Debra just out of spite and frustration.

It was Rose who thought of it first.

"Malcolm, stop!"

They all stopped and turned to face Rose.

"Mr. how well is this wolf trained?"

Immediately, Chambers knew what was needed. Kneeling beside Rage, he dipped his hand in some of the blood and passed it under the dog's nose.

"Get him!" he yelled.

Like a bolt of lightning, the wolf tore away and disappeared in seconds.

Meadows broke free of the forest and into open ground.  He had heard the baying of the wolf minutes earlier but still had not realized the animal was after him.  Clarisse had heard it too and ran out on the porch.  As soon as she saw Meadows, she began to look frantically for a weapon.  And there it was, Malcolm's gun still lying on the ground where it had been tossed.

Meadows was getting dizzy, but he was still clear enough to recognize Clarisse as she came off the porch.  How

or why didn't make any difference.  He had to get to her
before the others got to him.  And then he heard the howl
and turned.  The big wolf had cleared the woods and was on a
dead run toward him.  Meadows stumbled but stayed up and
began running for his life.  As he closed the distance to the
cabin, he now saw that Clarisse held something in her hand
and was standing with her legs apart.  If he hadn't been
seconds from death, he would have laughed.  She had
Malcolm's gun.  Lowering his head, he lurched forward and
with only feet between him and Clarisse she began firing.  She
didn't know how many times she pulled the trigger, but she
pulled it until she realized it had quit firing.  The wolf arrived
almost at the same time, and by the third shot he had pulled
the dead man's body to the ground and proceeded to rip out
his throat.

They all had heard the gun shots.  If there was any way
that a human could run faster, Malcolm put his two hundred
fifty-pound frame into a higher gear.  As he broke through the
woods and into the clearing, he saw Clarisse standing over a
form lying on the ground with the wolf standing beside her.
She was in shock.  Malcolm took the gun from her hand and
tilted her face, so he could look in her eyes.

"Clarisse, it's me, Malcolm."

Slowly, recognition began to sink in; and she put her
arms around him.

"It's okay, it's over."

They were both sitting on the porch when the others ran up.  Rose and Chambers went immediately inside to check on Debra.  She was frightened but okay.  Chambers knelt and introduced himself as Rose rounded up the water and cup.  Clarisse leaned over and kissed Malcolm on the cheek and walked inside.  Malcolm took one last look at what was left of Meadows and followed her.

"Who has a cell phone?" said Malcolm.

Rose pulled hers from the backpack.

Clarisse and Chambers both looked questioningly wondering what he was about to do.  He walked back outside.

———————

Arnie didn't recognize the number.  The FBI had arrived with nearly fifty agents and combined with the rangers there were seventy-five lawmen combing the woods looking for a jumper, Meadows, and now a missing detective.

"Arnie, it's me.  I need you to listen carefully.  I'll explain everything later.  Can anyone overhear this conversation?"

Arnie began to veer away from the closest searcher.

"Go ahead, Malcolm. "

"Debra Nix is alive.  Meadows is dead.  And I need you to get Tim Nix away from the group, so I can talk to him.  And I need you to do that now.  I'll stay by the phone."

Malcolm hung up knowing that Arnie would do what was asked.  It took nearly five agonizing minutes before the phone rang.

"Mr. Nix, did Arnie tell you your wife was alive?"

"Yes, God! yes, where is she?"

"I need for you to call your office and get access to a life flight helicopter.  Give them whatever story you have to.  When you get in the chopper, call me; and I'll give you the coordinates to get here.  Don't ask questions.  It's imperative that you do exactly as I say.  Now hand the phone back to my partner."

"Malcolm, the regional director of the FBI is here along with fifty agents.  Captain Edwards is here.  Hell, in another hour there will be a hundred National Guard arriving.  You want to give me a hint as to what you're doing?"

"There's too much to tell you, Arnie.  I know I'm asking you to put your butt on the line here and maybe even your career."

"Just tell me what you need for me to do."

In a few minutes, Malcolm hung up the phone and turned to see Clarisse and Chambers standing on the porch.

"Do I need to start running?" said Chambers.

"Not yet," said Malcolm.

Malcolm knelt and started to go through Meadows' bloody clothes.  There were several odds and ends, but he found what he had hoped was still there.  The wallet had several thousand dollars in it along with a picture ID.  It was a driver's license issued to Lawrence Lewis, who lived at 2230 Briar Ave., Boulder, Colorado.  Malcolm searched through the rest of the clothing but found nothing.

"You got anything that would prove you are Royse Chambers in the cabin.  Anything, pictures, something with your name on it, key chain...."

"My wedding ring.  It has my first initial and last name spelled out on the inside."

"Let me see it," said Malcolm.

Chambers went back inside and got the ring.  Malcolm looked at it is remembering all the burn victims whose bodies had been found with jewelry undamaged by the fire.

"Do you trust me, Royse?"

"Yes."

Malcolm placed the ring on Meadows' finger.

"Now we need to get Debra out of the cabin."

They all went back inside and made preparations to get the injured woman outside.  While that was being done, Malcolm told her Tim was on his way with a helicopter.  With

Debra safely outside and away from the cabin, Malcolm took Royse aside.

"You know what I'm about to do?"

"Yes, get yourself arrested for aiding and abetting a fugitive."

Malcolm smiled.

"Well, that may be true.  But if God is keeping count, you're up five to three on saving and taking lives.  Now where is the money?"

Chambers walked around the cabin and pulled the backpack out from under a rock.

With Chambers help, they dragged Meadows' body inside the cabin and set it on fire.

In about an hour, there was nothing left of the cabin but smoldering ashes.  Malcolm's phone rang.  He walked away knowing it was Nix.  In a few minutes, he came back and motioned Chambers to follow him.

"They'll be here in about five minutes."

Turning to Chambers, he said, "And you're going with 'em."

Malcolm held up his hand to stop any protest.

"You told me you trusted me."

Chambers nodded.

"When you get to the hospital take a taxi to the airport and buy yourself a ticket to Boulder.  When you get there, buy a disposable phone, and call me.  Here's the numbers for my partner and me.  I will fax you a birth certificate.  That's all you'll need to get a new social security card and driver's license.  Don't shave or cut your hair till you get to Colorado.  You also might want to get some clothes before you go to the airport."

Malcolm handed him three thousand dollars and the ID.

Tears had started to stream down Chambers' face. Malcolm turned, so they wouldn't have to look at each other.

"I'll make sure Rage is taken care of."

The sound of the chopper ended the conversation. Malcolm knew that time was of the essence.  The Calvary would have spotted the chopper and be headed this way. With little fanfare, a gurney suddenly appeared with two EMT's.  Debra was safely loaded in the helicopter.  As Chambers climbed in, Malcolm handed the backpack to Nix; and then turned to the girls and said, "Get in!"

They both looked at each other.

"How are you going to explain how you found this place, Clarisse?" said Malcolm.  "Get in, now!  Both of you!"

They reluctantly climbed in.  As the helicopter lifted and flew away, Chambers looked out the window and looked at the charred remains of the last ten years of his life.  He placed his face in his hands.

"Detective McBride is a remarkable man."

Chambers and the girls looked up to see Tim Nix sitting beside his wife holding her hand.

"Yes, he is," said Chambers.

"According to him, Debra would be dead if it hadn't been for you."

"She's pretty tough.  I'm not sure I did all that much."

"Don't kid yourself, Mr. Chambers.  According to Detective McBride, a lot of people would be dead if not for you."

"I've taken lives too."

"Yes, we've all made mistakes, sometimes terrible ones.  But if there's one thing I've learned from this ordeal, God has a plan for all of us.  And his plan was to put you in the path of a cold-blooded killer and stop him."

Within a few minutes, the helicopter came to rest atop the hospital helipad.  Interns were waiting as soon as the door opened.  As Debra Nix was being lowered to the ground, she told them to stop.  She painfully held out her hand motioning for Chambers to come over.  He bent over, and she put her hand behind his head and pulled him down to her face.

"Thank you, and may God bless and keep you wherever you go."

He stared as they opened the door and took her inside.  Nix said a few words to the girls, and they quickly went through the door. He then walked over to Chambers and offered his hand.

"I would have given Meadows anything he wanted for the safe return of my wife.  Two million dollars would have been a drop in the bucket for what Lacy and my company are worth.  I hope this will give you the fresh start you need."

He handed Chambers the backpack and sprinted away before anything more could be said.

# A HEAVY PRICE TO PAY

## CHAPTER NINETEEN

Like a kicked-over fire ant mound, the clearing was soon covered with agents and rangers.  Malcolm sat quietly with Rage who was having a seizure trying to figure out who to bite first.

"You McBride?"  said an overweight, gray headed, bespectacled, and obviously irritated man.

"That would be me," said Malcolm.

"You're under arrest."

Turning to an agent beside him he said, "Get him in cuffs."

"And who might you be?" said Malcolm standing up.

"Harvey Rhodes, Regional Director of the FBI.  And you are under arrest for the aiding and abetting of fugitive Royse Chambers."

"I need a minute," said Malcolm.

"You don't get crap!"

"That wolf over there will tear somebody's throat out if you don't let me talk to him."

"Agent Sims, if that animal moves, shoot it."

Malcolm began to walk over to Rage even as he was told several times to stop.  He knelt and placed his arms around the big wolf.

"I made a promise, but I thought I'd have more time. You're on you're on now.  Take care of yourself."

The big wolf stared as if in a daze, not understanding what to do. He whined as Malcolm stood up. Malcolm made the hand signal he'd seen Chambers do several times; the signal to tell Rage to leave.  The big wolf turned his head toward the trees, looked back at Malcolm, and trotted away.

———————

Arnie sat across a table staring at Malcolm in handcuffs.

"Royse call?" said Malcolm.

"Yes, he's pretty upset about you being in jail."

"Why did you feel a need to tell him?"

"I didn't have to tell him, Malcolm.  He knew.  How in God's name were you going to explain everything to the satisfaction of the NYPD much less the FBI?  And God help you, even if Captain Edwards figures out how to clean up this mess, Internal Affairs is waiting with an axe."

Malcolm leaned back and stared at the ceiling.

"Were you able to help with the birth certificate?"

"He's got it."

Malcolm stared down at the floor for several seconds.

"You know, Arnie, after Denise died, I felt like a ship without a keel.  As close a friend as you've always been, there was just no way I could make you feel or understand what I faced each and every day.  And then, like right before the sun begins to rise in the morning, bits and pieces of my soul started to come back.  Clarisse showed up.  A child with the same grit and fire that had sustained Denise through all the heartaches she experienced married to me.  And Rose.... We saved her, Arnie, but she saved me not only from Meadows, but by the joy I've had of watching her grow into a woman...."

He stopped for a minute and looked around the room.

"Royse Chambers.  You were right about him.  How does the quote go, 'Ours is not to reason why, ours is but to do or die.'?"

Malcolm smiled and clasped his hands staring at the cuffs.

"I've looked into the soulless abyss of the most horrible of predators and wondered why God would allow such men to walk among us?"

He sighed and looked at Arnie.

"I have no lawful excuse for what I've done and no will to fight it.  You are my brother, but I'm telling you to get as far away from me as you can.  The powers behind this are formidable, and they will take down everything and anybody that gets in their way.  You have a career to protect and a family to support.  Don't do anything to jeopardize that."

"Guard!"

Before Arnie could say a thing, Malcolm reached across the table and grabbed his hand.

"No touching!" yelled the guard.

"Not touching," said Malcolm.  "Just saying goodbye to my brother."

# RELENTLESS

## CHAPTER TWENTY

Clarisse and Rose had gotten a woman at the restaurant to let them borrow her car.  With a twelve-year-old behind the wheel, they got Rose's car from where they'd hidden it and got back home.  At almost the same time, two FBI agents showed up at Rose's apartment to ask them about Malcolm.  They had no knowledge of anyone named Royse Chambers.  After nearly an hour of constant effort to trip them up, the agents left.

————————

Malcolm sat in an interrogation room almost identical to the one at the two-four.  An Agent named Winters had a folder in front of him reading and referring to it.

"Okay, now let's go through this again.  You state that around midnight on the eleventh, you went outside the ranger station to get some fresh air.  At that time, you knew that Meadows was around?"

"Yes," said Malcolm.

"Pretty foolish, don't you think?"

"I made the assumption that even assholes have to sleep."

"You think this is funny, Detective?"

"Not in the least, Agent Winters."

"You've also stated that you saw a light.  Is that correct?"

"Yes."

"What did you do next?"

"As you can see by my statement, I began to follow it."

"Knowing Meadows was out there, you didn't think it prudent to get help?"

"I decided that by the time I got help whoever it was would be gone."

"What did you do next?"

"I continued to follow the light through some heavy underbrush for over an hour.  It came out in a clearing where I saw a cabin."

"Why did you not go back and get help at this point?"

"I still wasn't sure who it was.  If it was a camper or someone with legal rights to be there, all I would have done was cause some hard feelings both with the authorities and the man that owned the cabin."

"Continue."

"I tried to get to the cabin quietly, but he had a large dog that I later realized was a wolf.  It alerted him that I was outside."

"What happened then?"

"I was pretty sure at this point that it wasn't Meadows.  I didn't know who it was.  When he opened the door, I could see a woman inside lying on a crude bed of some sort.  I identified myself as a detective with the NYPD and asked him who he was.  That's when he pulled a gun and shot at me.  I was reluctant to return fire, but I did."

"You fired into the cabin knowing there was a woman inside?"

"Yes, I didn't know if it was a hostage or accomplice; but in fear of my own life, I returned fire and retreated behind some rocks."

"Why at this point did you not go for help?"

"Again, if I left, there was a good chance whoever it was would not be there when we got back."

"Go ahead."

"I waited nearly three hours until dawn making sure the male suspect didn't leave the cabin.  He opened the door and called out.  He had a comatose woman inside that he'd found in the forest and brought to the cabin.  He was willing to let me come in and take the woman outside."

"And you believed him?"

"He sounded sincere, yes."

"Go ahead."

"I laid my gun down where he could see it, and he did the same.  We both went inside and carried the woman out and laid her on the ground.  I covered her with animal hides that he had in the cabin, and I made her as comfortable as I could."

"What next?"

"The suspect went back inside the house.  I tried to convince him to come out, but he refused.  I told him help was coming; and in a few minutes, I saw flames inside the cabin.  Then I heard what sounded like a shotgun blast.  I ran up to the cabin door and opened it.  The suspect was lying dead on the floor with his face and head blown away, and the cabin about to be engulfed in flames.  I just had enough time to get back outside."

"And what about the money?"

"I never saw any money.  The suspect brought out a backpack with the woman, but all that was in it was a cell phone and some clothing."

"So, you called the woman's husband before your own partner and the others at the ranger station?"

"Yes."

"How did you know who he was?"

"She regained consciousness and told me about an hour after the cabin burned down.  She told me to look in her bag for her phone.  I could see she was in serious condition, but I felt like her husband had the resources to help her the quickest and therefore should be the first to know that she was alive."

"You're lying through your teeth, Detective.  First, when the autopsy comes back, it will be Jarvis Meadows in the cabin.  And as soon as Mrs. Nix is given the green light to talk, she'll confirm it.  The only question now is where is Chambers and the money?  There is only one reason why you would have kept your partner and everyone else out of the loop.  You and Chambers are going to split the money."

Malcolm almost laughed.  He bit his lip to keep it from happening, but the absurd way that Winters had come up with why Malcolm would have protected a fleeing felon was comical.  There was a tap on the one-way glass, and Winters gathered up his papers and left the room.  Malcolm couldn't count the number of times he'd stood on the opposite side of a window just like that and watched an interrogation.  He figured that at the very least there were five men in the room.  Knowing they would let him "sweat" for awhile, he laid his head down on the table and closed his eyes.

"We've got nobody to dispute his story except Debra Nix," said Agent Rhodes.

"We don't even have that, Sir," said Agent Peters. "Agent Winters here doesn't know it, but she was deposed this morning.  She verifies everything the detective said."

"It's bull shit," said Lincoln of Internal Affairs.  "The guy's worse than a Teflon Skillet.  How much longer on the autopsy?"

"Tomorrow or the next day at the latest," said Rhodes. "Our people are handling it.   Now, get him out here and back to his cell."

———————

"They have the finest Forensic Scientists in the country working on this.  A ring on a finger is not gonna fool 'em, Malcolm."

Arnie sat at the table and watched Malcolm pace the room.  He was a lot more upset than Malcolm.

"Arnie, whatever happens next is something neither one of us can control.  You, Clarisse, Rose, even Mrs. Nix, need to keep your mouths shut.  Anything you say will only implicate that you were complicit in all of this."

Arnie understood.  Anything they said would only hurt not help.  But the frustration of knowing the reasons behind Malcolm's actions only made the secret harder to bear.

"Have the girls been to see you?"

"Yes, I told them to stay away, which I also told you, but like the rebel you are...."

"I think the word you used was brother."

"That too," laughed Malcolm.

Malcolm finally sat down and began to inspect a room that he'd already seen three times.

"You remember that guy with the Arabic name that we caught jay walking?  It was twenty degrees, and he was walking back and forth trying to toughen up his feet."

"Mohammed," said Arnie.

"Yeah, that was the guy.  Wonder where he is now?  And then there was the guy we caught marching up and down an alley with a rusty old gun protecting a cat and her kittens.  We've seen some pretty weird stuff, haven't we?"

Arnie listened as Malcolm continued to rattle off at least a dozen more instances after which he would always say, 'I just love this job.'  It made Arnie smile and made him sad.

"You haven't told Sheryl anything have you?" said Malcolm.

"No, she and the baby are still in Houston."

"If and when this thing goes to trial, I'll call her.  If she were here now, she would just sit around and worry like the rest of you.  She's got my grandchild and law school to deal with.  I appreciate you and Maxine not telling her."

"Maxine is just as worried as I am."

"Time's up," said the guard.

---

Later that afternoon, the Assistant District Attorney, Elton Roberts, came down to Malcolm's cell and delivered the news.

"The body has been identified as Jarvis Meadows.  Is there anything about your statement you want to change?"

Malcolm knew that was the final nail in his coffin.

"Nope," he said.  "You have my statement."

# AND THEN THERE WAS LIGHT

## CHAPTER TWENTY-ONE

There's a story that most elementary children read about a baseball player named Casey.  He was supposedly the greatest hitter of all time and lived in a small community called Mudville.  In the final game, which today would be called the Seventh Game of the World Series, it was the bottom of the ninth with two out.  Casey had allowed the pitcher to throw two strikes and never lifted the bat off his shoulder.  He only needed one pitch.  That's how confident he was.  But when that pitch was thrown, he missed it.  The account of his failure at the plate was followed by the statement, "There is no joy in Mudville ."

The trial lasted two days.  Malcolm took the stand in his own defense but failed to rebut one question.  There was no way the ring could have gotten on Meadows' finger unless Malcolm had put it there.  That ring also meant that Malcolm had killed Meadows and disposed of the body.  The case had now gone to the jury.  As open and shut as it had seemed to the prosecutor, it apparently was not that easy for the jury.  They had obviously been moved by Malcolm's care for Debra Nix and his determination for her husband to be the first one on the scene.  Still, the money and Royse Chambers were missing, and the only logical conclusion was that Malcolm knew where both were.  Arnie had decided he had to call Sheryl.  She and Malcolm Junior sat behind Malcolm along with Arnie, Maxine, Clarisse, and Rose.  After six hours, the jury sent word that they had finally reached a verdict.  Malcolm's attorney had mysteriously disappeared for nearly the whole time.  Everyone assumed he was with the DA trying to cut a deal.  As the jury filed back into court, the defense attorney suddenly appeared and went directly to the prosecutor's table.  A loud interchange ensued, and the judge called both to approach the bench.  More arguments erupted, and it became heated right in front of the jury and the entire courtroom.  The judge called for a ten-minute recess and hauled both attorneys back to his chambers.  The ten minutes turned into almost an hour.  Finally, the doors to the judge's chambers opened, and they all filed out.

"Ladies and gentlemen of the jury I realize that you have reached a verdict.  But new evidence has just been presented in my chambers directly relating to the innocence of the accused.  Although this is completely out of order at this late date, in the interest of justice, I'm going to allow this evidence to be presented now and in open court.  The prosecutor will have the right to cross examine.  Bailiff, bring Royse Chambers into court."

The shock on the faces in the courtroom was as if a bomb had gone off, but none more profound than on Malcolm's face.

Royse Chambers entered wearing a bright blue suit.  He was clean shaven and wearing shoes that shined.  He walked down the aisle, through the gate, and up to the witness stand.

"Mr. Chambers, you swear that the testimony you're about to give is the truth, the whole truth, and nothing but the truth so help you God?"

"I do," said Chambers.

"Please state your full name for the court."

"My name is Royse Collin Chambers."

"Mr. Chambers you are a federal fugitive suspected in the murders of three people almost ten years ago.  Is that correct?"

"Yes."

"Has any deal been offered you for this testimony?"

"No."

"Very well.  Will you please tell the court the sequence of events that transpired on the night of May 11?"

"I was in front of my cabin, and I saw someone jump out of a plane.  The chute only partially opened, and I watched the jumper plummet into the trees.  More out of curiosity than anything else, I went to the area and found the jumper.  It was a woman and by some miracle she was still alive.  I learned later her name was Debra Nix.  She was badly injured, so I made a travois out of her parachute and took her back to the cabin.  She had a backpack with her which at that time I didn't know held over two million dollars.

Apparently, a man by the name of Jarvis Meadows was waiting to collect a ransom from Mrs. Nix's husband.  He must have seen me and followed me back to the cabin.  I have no idea why he didn't attack me before I reached the cabin.  Nevertheless, when I got Mrs. Nix back to the cabin, he showed up.  By that time, I had found the money and was determined to keep it.  I had no idea what to do with Mrs. Nix, but I had no plans to kill her.  I had a wolf that I raised from a pup.  The wolf alerted me to Meadows' presence.  Being a wanted man, I had a weapon; and I was ready to use it.  When he burst through the door, I shot him with my twelve gauge.  Before I could clean up and dispose of the body, the wolf alerted me that someone else was outside.  I looked outside and saw that man, pointing at Malcolm, approaching the cabin."

"Let the record show that Mr. Chambers is indicating the accused, Malcolm McBride."

"So, ordered," said the Judge.

"Continue," said the Attorney.

"He was armed.  I told him there was an injured woman inside.  We called a temporary truce, so we could get her out.  The detective had not seen Meadows' body.  With the woman safely outside, I got an idea.  I asked the detective to wait outside.  I went back in the cabin and put my wedding band on Meadows' hand. With the detective still outside I closed and locked the door. I picked up the shotgun and shot Meadows in the face so there could be no identification.  I set the cabin on fire.  When I built the cabin, I made a crawl space for an escape just in case I was ever discovered."

"So, let me be clear, Mr. Chambers.  You took off your ring and placed it on Meadows' hand. You then shot him in the face making Detective McBride believe that you had just committed suicide.  You then set the cabin on fire and escaped through a trap door?"

"A crawl space, but yes sir, that's what happened. "

"Mr. Chambers this is important so please answer carefully and clearly.  At any time was Detective McBride aware that the body of Jarvis Meadows was in the cabin?"

"No, Sir."

"At any time was Detective McBride aware that there was two million dollars in the cabin?"

"No, Sir."

"At any time did you tell Detective McBride who you were or that you were an escaped felon?"

"I don't know if he figured out who I was.  I didn't care. I was not going back with him or anybody else."

"Mr. Chambers you do realize that at the end of this trial you will be arrested and tried for the murders of three people?"

"Yes."

"So, I'm at a loss as to why you would surrender yourself to save a man that you only met once and who was there to arrest you?"

"I couldn't let an innocent man pay for something I'd done. I've had time to do a lot of thinking in the last ten years. I destroyed the lives of three people along with their families. I just couldn't live with it anymore."

"One last thing, Mr. Chambers. Where's the money?"

"I gave it back Mr. Tim Nix yesterday."

"If it please the court, Mr. Nix is in the courtroom today and will testify that he has received the money as Mr. Chambers stated. That's all your Honor. I'm finished with the witness."

"Mr. Roberts, you may cross examine," said the Judge.

From the moment Chambers began to testify, Elton Roberts and his team had been frantically passing papers back and forth. Now they were all at the table with their heads in one big pile.

"Mr. Roberts, do you have any questions for this witness?"

"Only one your Honor.  Mr. Chambers under oath do you swear other than the night Jarvis Meadows was killed, that you have never seen Detective McBride before?"

Without hesitation, he answered.  I've never seen him before."

Roberts went back to the table and sat down.

"Your Honor, in light of this new evidence, I ask that the court drop all charges against my client."

"Any objections, Mr. Roberts?"

"No, your Honor."

"Very well.  All the charges against the accused or hereby declared null and void.  Detective McBride, you are a free man."

As the courtroom exploded, Malcolm never took his eyes off Royse Chambers.  Within seconds, the Bailiffs had him handcuffed and hauled out of the courtroom.  Clarisse climbed over the rail and put Malcolm in a headlock; Rose was soon wrapped around his waist, and Arnie, Maxine, and Sheryl patiently waited for their turns.  When they all finally headed toward the door, Malcolm saw Captain Edwards, and Steven Barrett, Malcolm's attorney, in deep discussion.

"Let me speak to these guys for a minute," said Malcolm.  "I'll meet you outside."

"Congratulations," said Captain Edwards extending his hand.

"Thanks, Captain," said Malcolm.

Steven Barrett extended his hand which Malcolm took with both of his.

"Did he call you?" said Malcolm looking at Barrett.

"No, he called me," said Captain Edwards.  "He didn't say how he knew you were in trouble, and I didn't ask him.  I told him the situation, and he told me to pick him up at the airport.  I called Steven and told him to delay the verdict anyway he could, but he didn't have to.  The jury did that for him by taking so long to decide.  I just barely got him to the courthouse.  After that, it was up to Steven to get him on the stand.  It also didn't hurt that you had a sympathetic judge willing to break protocol."

Malcolm shook his head.

"You've still got to deal with Internal Affairs," said Captain Edwards.  "There's a good chance you'll be suspended."

"For how long?" said Malcolm.

"Thirty days without pay, but I'm sure the women outside will be glad to feed you."

Malcolm thanked them both again and walked outside.

# TWO WEEKS LATER

Malcolm sat across from a man about to serve twenty-five years to life in a Federal Penitentiary.

"I know you're in turmoil over this," said Chambers.

Malcolm had been staring at the table but looked up.

"Don't be," said Chambers.  "I've learned a lot of things. I told the judge it was over a period of ten years.  Actually, it was more like six months.  I learned compassion, loyalty, integrity, and most of all, love.  I thought I knew and possessed all these things; but you, Clarisse, and even the Nix's showed me I had nothing.  You all awakened me to the fact that all we have is what's right in front of us.  There is no tomorrow.  Do you know what the Nix's did with the money?"

Malcolm shook his head.

"They opened a Trust Fund for the children of the two men I killed and gave a half-million to the husband of the woman whose life I took.  It won't heal their wounds, but it was a gesture that the Nix's felt needed to be made on my behalf.  Clarisse and Rose have been here to see me.  I got to meet your partner and his wife.  I'm surrounded by good people, Malcolm.  And most important, I've finally made peace with myself.  I want you to do the same.  We've both got our lives back.  Wherever I go and whatever I'm required to do, I'll do it."

Chambers stood up and the two men embraced.  The guard didn't say a word.

# EPILOG

Arnie and Malcolm were sitting at their desks after visiting Debra Nix at the hospital.

"I wonder what it would really be like to commit suicide by jumping out of an airplane?" said Arnie.

Malcolm looked up from his computer.

"Do what?"

"I don't know.  I just wondered?"

"And I've always wondered what it would be like to get hit in the head with a pickaxe," said Malcolm.

Arnie Ignored Malcolm's attempt at sarcasm.

"My birthday's Saturday.  I just wondered what it would feel like to free fall ten thousand feet?" said Arnie.

"Let me answer that for you, good buddy.  First, as soon as you jump out, you're going to scream, 'O crap!'  Then comes the need for a change of underwear, which you won't have to worry about in another sixty seconds if the chute doesn't open.  And then as good old mother earth rushes up to meet you, you'll have just enough time to say to yourself, 'What the hell was I thinking!'"

"So, you would never do anything like that?" said Arnie.

"Let me tell you a story," said Malcolm.  "There once was a sparrow that refused to fly south for the winter.  The other sparrows tried to get him to go, but he just wouldn't. Winter came, and the sparrow got cold, real cold.  He started freezing and said to himself, 'To heck with this, I'm going south'.  But he'd waited too long.  He hadn't flown very far when his wings started to ice over, and he crash landed.  Now, he was cold and couldn't even move.  Suddenly, a cow came along and crapped on him.  The crap was warm, and it helped to thaw the sparrow.  Then a cat came along and spotted the sparrow in the crap and started to lick him clean.  The sparrow couldn't believe his luck.  After the cat licked the sparrow clean, he ate the sparrow.  There are three morals to this story:  One, not everyone that craps on you is your enemy.  Two, not everyone that cleans you up and helps you get out of the crap is your friend.  Three, if you know you're in crap but your happy, stay there."

Arnie thought for a few seconds.

"What did that have to do with me jumping out of an airplane?"

"You mean it didn't make sense to you?"

"Not a bit."

"I rest my case."

# COMING SOON:

# SIMPER FI

## A MCBRIDE-BUCKHOLTZ NOVEL

# CHAPTER 1

## WRONG PLACE - WRONG TIME

Arnie was drinking coffee when the man walked in. Dressed in military fatigues, Arnie thought he might be a Marine, but it was hard to tell anymore.

"He gives me the creeps," said Rose Marie as she filled Arnie's cup.

"How so?" said Arnie.

"This is the third day he's come in.  He sits in the same corner and orders a cup of coffee."

"With the exception of doing it three days in a row, I'm doing the same thing," said Arnie.

"It's not the same and you know it."

She stood there with hands on her hips glaring across the room.  Arnie had to smile.  Rose Marie Shaffer was a country girl from the Texas backwoods who could smell trouble a mile away.  She'd been raised in a cult from which Arnie and his partner, Detective Malcolm McBride, had rescued her.  It was a long story that had almost cost Malcolm and Arnie their lives.

"Well?" said Rose Marie now glaring at Arnie.

Arnie looked back at the man.

"Well, what?" he said.

"You're impossible."  And she walked over to the next booth to refill coffee.

Arnie could see what looked like several medals pinned to the man's chest.  Assuming he was a soldier, he looked young to have served enough time to get that many awards. He looked to be in his twenty's, but in war there was no age limit on bravery.  As the soldier leaned back in his chair, Arnie could see the polished boots and the gun.  It was illegal to carry a weapon in public without a permit, and Arnie was sure the military wasn't handing those out.  Malcolm McBride would have simply walked over, flashed his shield, and demand to know the guy's name and why he carrying a weapon in a public restaurant?  Course Malcolm didn't have a tactful bone in his body.

As Arnie continued to watch, the restaurant door opened. The soldier pulled out the gun and laid it on the table. Rose Marie was across the room right in Arnie's line of sight, and she saw it too.  Before Arnie could get up, three men in suits walked in, and as if that had been the cue, all hell broke loose.

___________

"So, you thought the best solution at the time was to just shoot him?"

Detective Malcolm McBride was in an interrogation room with Memphis Starnes who had murdered her husband.

"Seemed so," she said.

"How long were you two married?"

"Never married."

"How long did you live together?"

"Thirty-three years."

"And all of a sudden you decided to get married last week?"

There was no response.

"Okay, now let me try to understand this.  You lived with Stan Starnes for thirty-three years.  You decided to marry him last week, and then yesterday he did something or said something that was so bad you felt a need to shoot him?"

"Yes."

Malcolm paused for a few seconds to give Memphis a chance to tell him why she killed him.  She didn't.

"Why?"

"Why what?"

"Why did you kill him?"

"You married, Detective?"

The remembrance of Denise's murder immediately sprang to the surface.  It was all Malcolm could do to maintain his composure.

"My wife passed away."

"Any children?"

"I have a daughter and a grandchild."

"If your wife came in one night in a drunken stupor and told you that thirty-two years ago, she had smothered your child because it wouldn't stop crying, what would you do?"

Malcolm was stunned.  There was no way he saw that coming.  Every motive in the world had crossed his mind but that one.  Before he could respond, the door opened.  It was captain Edwards.

"Detective.  There's been a shooting at a restaurant on 42nd.  Arnie's hurt."